DEEPER THAN HELL

JOSHUA MILLICAN

Cover Art and Design by Christian Francis.

Author photo by Ama Lea.

To see more great titles, please visit www.encyclopocalypse.com.

Encyclopocalypse Publications
www.encyclopocalypse.com

For you, Leon. Try not to get stuck in holes.
-JM

DREW'S MAP

LAS VEGA[S]

THE WEB

THE TUNN[EL]

ACOLYTES

TABERNA[L]
CITY

THE GREAT

SPC
O6[...]

BEL[...]
OGR[E]

BOTTOM[...]
WONDER
LAND

BAC[K]
ROOMS

XANA[...]

INNER
OCEAN

CHAPTER ONE

THE THING MOST PEOPLE don't understand about Heroin is this:

It's not about the quality of pleasure. It's about the absence of pain.

People will say I'm a selfish fuck who traded my friends, family, and future for a transient rush. But pleasure is just the bait on the hook. The real magic of Heroin is how it makes all my fears and anxieties, no matter how crippling, dissolve into Warm Oblivion.

"But it's killing you," some people will say.

Even before I was a junkie, I always imagined I'd die young. Not because I want to. I'm terrified of dying to tell you the truth. It's more like a premonition.

Some people will say Heroin is my way of committing suicide slowly. But maybe Heroin has been my cure for suicide. Some people say, "Turn to God." But "Heroin is my God" is what I'd say. That's why I always capitalize Heroin when I write about it. Reverence.

But now, I'm about to meet God. Real God. Superior to all the other Gods.

Back up.

I've always been unusually susceptible to the ravages of non-physical pain, but nothing mattered after I buried the plunger. Not the bullies who beat me or the teachers who never gave a fuck. Not the beautiful liars who gaslit me, swearing they were true and I must be crazy for being so insanely jealous. Not the devastation of treachery among friends, or infiltrators practicing divide and conquer. Not the lust of money that seems to trump loyalty at every turn, the backroom dealings and inter-tribal gerrymandering. Not the guilt of never living up to my parents' expectations, the taunting torture of missed opportunities, or the never-ending punishment of regret. The permanence of grudges, the inability to let sleeping dogs lie, the abject terror of looking at my face in the mirror... None of it matters in the Warm Oblivion, that netherworld of waking dreams and dreamless sleep.

Warm Oblivion is more than just a feeling. It's more than just being high. It's more than just a state of mind. Warm Oblivion is a destination, Nirvana manifested, a reverse cocoon that envelopes the gray concrete and foul odors of reality, delivering the purest pulchritude. It's a place that makes all the promised joys of Heaven pale, a place that turns the promise of Heaven itself into Purgatory, and from the moment I arrived, I knew I was home.

When my allotted time expired, nothing mattered except getting back.

The incriminating abscesses, the weight loss, the sunken eyes, even the subtle reek of slow decay... I could care less. Life outside of Warm Oblivion is Hell and Heroin keeps a tidal wave of emotional agony at bay.

I make my way in Las Vegas. Sin City gives me everything I need. Random circumstances brought me here, but it all seems inevitable on reflection. Vegas is perfect for disappearing. Perfect for completely divorcing myself from the restrictions of civilized society. An ideal destination for emotional suppression.

Vegas is perfect for scavenging. I collect abandoned coins from slot machines, chips dropped on casino floors, forgotten ATM cards, misplaced purses, and backpacks. Resources abound if you look for them. There's a symbiosis to it all, and I sometimes feel like I was legitimately foraging through my natural habitat. The Gods of Vegas understand junkies are an inevitable byproduct of vice, and that we play a vital role in this ecosystem. Like insects who clear debris from the forest floors.

It's never taken me more than a day to scrape together enough scratch for a fat wad of tar and a 2-liter bottle of Mt. Dew—and that's all I really need at night.

I was one of hundreds living in the tunnels and storm drains beneath the city. It's an intricate system built to protect casinos and hotels from flash flooding. A lot of cities have them. Media attention turned this particular zone into something of a countercultural hotspot, attracting all kinds of temporary residents:

Guerilla campers, Burning Man devotees, Slab City evictees, neo hobos, college dropouts, conspiracy theorists, teenage utopists, economic refugees, anarchist affinities, punk rock collectives, parole violators, urban explorers, and repeat alien abductees (among others).

The population thinned when the economy hit an upswing, but the infrastructure remained: An active subterranean shantytown for the full-timers. There's a guy who fixes shoes, and a guy who recharges batteries, and a guy who sells hoodies. There's a guy who always has extra belts and a guy who passes out cups of bleach. There's even a guy who sees to all your spiritual needs, should you have any.

Now let me tell you about Drew.

Drew was something of an anomaly and a celebrity in the tunnels. The first thing everybody noticed about him was his surprisingly upbeat attitude. Not what you'd expect from someone living in the hardcore fringes. We're a generally melancholic bunch. But Drew had a great personality and natural good looks, despite shooting as much Heroin as anyone I knew. Drew didn't beg, borrow, or steal, yet, somehow, he was never lacking in the necessities (those being Heroin and her corresponding paraphernalia). It was like magic.

He got checks twice a month from a PO Box he rented at Kinko's, but no one knew where they came from. There was a persistent rumor, probably started by Drew himself, that he'd been part of a one-hit-wonder band in the mid-2000's—or a boy band.

"They were huge overseas," someone told me. "Mostly in Japan and Korea."

Another popular theory was that he was on disability for a seizure disorder, a condition all but cured by his near constant Heroin use.

Other posited explanations included: Section 8 benefits, a secret trust fund, and payments for work as a police informant.

He'd been living underground for a while before I arrived, so I was lucky he took me under his wing. As easy as it is to fill your veins in Vegas, going solo is a dangerous game. It doesn't matter how big or intimidating you are, loners are easy targets (and I'm not big or intimidating). So, he had my back, and I had his, from day one. We'd watch for interlopers, share food, cut each other's hair—we'd even spoon on cold nights. We shared a hovel built out of plywood and discarded chain-link. It had a burn barrel out front, a couple of hammocks strung between the walls, and a crash mattress on the floor.

Every night, after slamming, Drew would tell me stories as we drifted off into Warm Oblivion. The blackness that surrounded us, the sick rainbows of spray-paint that covered every surface, would dissolve, melt, and reform into a cinematic panorama of his words. It was better than any movie, more engaging than the most profound works of literature.

"Hey Sonny, you ever heard of the Cave of Letters?" he asked me on my first night underground.

"Back in the 1st Century, the Romans went to the Holy Land to slaughter all the Jews, right, and they built this huge military out-post in the mountains. Now, just recently, archeologists discovered an opening under the city that led to an entire cave system. It turns out, this one tribe of Jews escaped underground to avoid the Romans—and no one knew about it! They found living quarters, and kitchens, and Temples, and even pens for livestock. They only found a few bodies, but at the deepest levels, they found passageways that had been completely sealed off.

"Now let me ask you this," Drew said, pausing for dramatic effect and to make sure I was paying attention. "Do you think all those people just died off or, maybe came up someplace else?"

I shrugged.

"Fuck no!" Drew countered. "Obviously, they moved down even deeper. And they sealed the tunnels so no one could follow them. It's possible to think they're still alive down there, all these generations later, completely removed from the surface. Don't you think so, Sonny?

Why wouldn't they be? They've probably evolved to life without the sun. They probably look different now. But I bet they're still there.

"Now think about this, Sonny…" There was another pause that knocked me out of my nod. "If archeologists just discovered the Cave of Letters a few years ago, how many other underground societies do you think are out there? That can't be the only one."

If Drew wasn't completely lost in his own Warm Oblivion, he'd slide seamlessly into another story, like: "Hey Sonny, did you know the Pyramids are as deep as they are tall?" or "Have you heard about the Rodent People of New York City?" or "Do you know the legend of the Minotaur?" or "Have you heard the myth of Persephone…" There were obvious central themes in Drew's stories, repeated tendrils that bound them, like the connective tissues of an anthology.

We lived in the open space about 150 yards down one of the main runoff channels, just south-east of the Strip. It's a sizable chamber, a convergence point for dozens of drainage pipes. At night refracted flashes of neon still manage to find their way inside.

It's mostly inhabited by other addicts, and we organized ourselves like tribes based on drug of choice.

Heroin heads and pill poppers just want a quiet, comfortable place to shoot and crash. We cluster along the east wall in a series of sheds and shanties. You can always find a lit burn barrel to warm up besides, or a couch to flop on. So many old couches have been dragged down there you could probably reconstruct Stonehenge with them.

Crackheads are generally older folks in their 40's and 50's. Cold War throwbacks from the pre-meth era. They keep to themselves for the most part, sometimes forming small circles to cook by campfire, or to watch sports on TV. Despite common stereotypes, crackheads are a generally mellow bunch. Still, a lot of people consider them subhuman or lost causes, irreparably damaged, feeble minded. Constantly picking up pebbles, more akin to animals or creatures than people, slaves to the strict commandments of a lesser god.

Meth heads make up the largest tribe by far, and it sucks because you really need to watch out for them. They never sleep, which means they never stop spinning. Some of them cook product, polluting the already stagnant air with nauseating plumes of sulfer and ammonia. Every other night's a nonstop cacophony of feuding, fighting, and fucking. Meth heads are prone to violence, exasperated by audio and visual hallucinations linked to sleep deprivation. Everything about them feels toxic. I've seen stabbings, rapes—even a full-fledged riot that sent us running for our lives amid gunshots and Molotov cocktail volleys.

The newest tribe on the rise is comprised of Spice addicts, aka the Face Eaters. Obviously, these fuckers scare the hell out of me. I once saw a guy worked into such a frenzy that he started running full speed into a wall. Over and over. Finally, when he was gushing from his nose and forehead, he backed-up for one last sprint, screaming like Braveheart as he charged the wall. And when he hit, there was this quick flash of dark blue lightning and the scent of afterburn—and he was gone. It was like he had just glitched-out. Like he just ran through the fucking wall, leaving a pulsating mass of blood, snot, and bile in a warped silhouette. Yeah, I was high at the time, but that's exactly what I saw. Heroin isn't a hallucinogen. There's something exceptionally insidious about Spice.

Chaos reaches critical levels periodically. But then, like clockwork, the floods come. It's like the Gods of Vegas simultaneously feel our plight and condemn our wickedness, sending roaring, baptismal waters as a means of purification.

The city gets an enema, and out comes months of shit. Actual shit, yes, but also thousands of used condoms, hundreds of shopping carts, tangles of clothes and needles, islands of debris, vermin (both dead and alive), and some things you don't even want to know about.

Inevitably, the floods push out a human body or two, sometimes fresh, sometimes skeletal, usually somewhere in between. Someone who overdosed in a corner and went unnoticed, or a well-stashed murder victim. Could have been me one day, if I had stayed.

Building a new shanty after flooding takes some effort, and usually means sleeping on cement for a few days. But there were times, in the immediate aftermath, when our spot felt fresh and spacious. Like a magical catacomb with fires casting shadows in every direction. Sometimes it got so quiet we heard voices coming from other tunnels miles away. Sometimes we heard music, both recognizable and otherworldly. Soon enough meth heads and the like would return to destroy our otherwise peaceful vibe—until the next big storm.

"Hey Sonny, you ever heard about the Prehistoric Superhighway?" Drew asked me as I slammed my plunger. I hadn't, but it didn't matter. Drew would continue either way.

"There are caves that go from Northern Ireland all the way to Turkey, and they've barely been explored. They're filled with torches, and tools, and paintings that go back to the Stone Ages."

In case you hadn't figured it out yet, Drew loved living underground. Like it was noble. Like he was connecting to a primitive and enlightened state of existence. A deliberate, spiritual lifestyle. This was his *Walden*.

"These tunnels right here, they lead to their own Superhighway." He'd point whimsically into the darkness, waving his finger in an infinity sign, leaving a golden trail and ethereal glitter. "You can get anywhere in the city, Sonny Boy. And that's just the beginning."

It had taken years to complete the networks under Vegas. Offices were built for construction supervisors and city planners, then abandoned when work in a particular sector wrapped up. Some of them even had bathrooms and sleeping quarters. Finding an empty office was like winning the lottery, but Drew considered himself lucky.

"I'll find us a place, Sonny Boy. A place with electricity, and running water, and a door to keep these crazy fuckers out of our business. We'll make a big score and shoot for days at a time, not a care in the world. We'll be set, Sonny Boy!"

I hated it when he called me "Sonny Boy." Not because he was five years younger than me, but because that's what my dad used to call me. I hated my dad.

I also loved it when Drew called me "Sonny Boy."

From the "front porch" of our shanty, the main tunnel's wide-open mouth looked about the size of a grapefruit. I liked that I could always see it, even after I kicked the preliminary jitters of living underground. I liked knowing the exit was there—just in case I needed it. It was a reminder that the world outside still existed, no matter how far into Warm Oblivion I drifted. I never wanted to go so far deep I couldn't see my way out.

Sometimes, after an especially big hit, I'd start getting literal tunnel vision. Like, black clouds gathering in my periphery, closing in. To keep from panicking, I'd focus on the entrance, like it was a beacon. And as long as I could see it everything would be okay. Sometimes, the clouds would get so thick that the opening was just a pin prick, a lone star in a pitch-black sky. Sometimes it felt like I was trapped in the icy grip of something paralytic, a succubus sucking the breath right out of me. Those times, when the haze finally receded, I'd be gasping for air and Drew (bless his heart) would be slapping my chest.

"Easy there, Sonny Boy! Don't you leave me, now!" He had an awesome smile, like a beacon.

Drew was infinitely more adventurous than I was. He'd go on days-long excursions underground, re-emerging with new stories to tell (and a strong hankering for Heroin).

He told me, for example, about a subway system that ran from the airport to Groom Lake and Area 51. He told me that some of the bigger, newer hotels had dozens of sublevels teeming with extremely illegal activities (like bestiality and live snuff), all catering to extremely wealthy psychopaths. He told me there was a mirror image of The Luxor, a reverse pyramid, directly below it, meaning the hotel is actually an 8-sided diamond.

Over the years, he'd come home with some doozies. Like, Satanic cults and white slavery circuits, drug factories and operating rooms for the surgical harvesting of organs, death merchants and serial killers. Even trolls—real, actual trolls! To be fair, Drew never claimed to have seen these things himself. Usually, it was something he'd heard from someone who'd been living underground since way back when. But Drew believed it—or at least he wanted to believe.

"There's some seriously crazy shit going on down there, Sonny Boy. Never doubt it."

Life naturally divides itself into chapters, but big events launch entirely new volumes. Drew and I were on one such precipice.

On the day before everything was divided into "Then" and "Now," I was sitting in a lawn chair on the "front porch," chin on my chest, enjoying some mid-afternoon W.O., when, someone kicked my foot. I fought through the confusion of semi-consciousness and focused on a white guy with cornrows in his hair, dressed in a track suit. He was talking to me.

"Are you talking to me?" I asked him, continuing to emerge from the Warm Oblivion.

"I said, 'Where the fuck is Drew at?'!"

Reflexively, I scanned the back of our shanty.

"He's not here," I told the guy who had a silver grill on his front teeth. The complete ensemble identified him as one of Thaddaeus's boys. Drew had previously explained that the "matching uniforms" made it harder for cops to pin specific crimes on specific goons, and someone was always willing to take a rap for Thaddaeus.

"Yeah, no shit, Sherlock!" From his vantage point, he could see perfectly well that I was alone. "When's he coming back?"

"I don't know." It was true, I didn't.

"You tell him Thaddaeus wants him topside now! Bellagio."

Thaddaeus and Enrique were the only two Heroin dealers in our little corner of Vegas. Enrique sold China White, catering almost exclusively to rock stars, actors, and socialites—above ground all the way. Thaddaeus was the dealer for the rest of us, a slinger of the "Cheap & Strong," a working-class businessman who held regular hours, selling out of his car. He'd park at different casinos on different days to mix things up, but his posse always knew where to find him (and they were easy to spot, another benefit of the unified dress code).

Drew got home a few hours later, somewhat out of breath.

"One of Thaddaeus's boys was looking for you."

"Oh yeah?"

"He said Thaddaeus wants to see you. He said meet him at the Bellagio." Drew sat down on the floor mat, pulled gear out of his pocket, and started prepping. It was as if what I just told him didn't even register. After a minute or so, I prodded: "So what's up with that, with Thaddaeus?"

"Fuck if I know."

"His boy seemed serious."

"Look, Sonny, I don't know what dude wants and I don't care. I'm almost ready to shoot. You coming?"

"Of course," I said, sitting down beside him to cook up my own. Back into the Warm Oblivion we dove. I remember it was a good batch, the kind that puts a sweet metallic tang in the back of your throat. Like pennies coated in honey. I slumped into weightlessness.

"You know what a vision quest is, Sonny? It's part of most Indigenous cultures: A coming of age ritual where a young man goes off by himself into the wilderness, sometimes after eating peyote. There was a tribe right around here that sent their young men on vision quests, but not into the desert. They went underground, into caves that ran beneath the mountains.

"And these teenagers, these kids, would spend days creeping downward. Sometimes, the corridors would be so tight, they'd have to crawl on their bellies. The only light was from these lamps that were just leaves filled with oil. They'd find these tight crevasses, barely big enough for a single person, and spend days creating elaborate paintings, knowing full well no other human eyes would ever see them. No human eyes. And they always painted the same thing: The Great God, The God of the Hunt with huge horns. The God of Meat!

"That's what I'm doing when I go down there, Sonny Boy. I'm on vision quests. I'm looking for God."

"Yo, mother fucking Drew!"

It was Thaddaeus, coming right towards us with three of his boys. I remember thinking the posse looked semi-comic, like a group of mismatched clones: Fat, tall, Chinese, Ginger, each sporting cornrows, track suits, and chrome grills.

"Why you been ducking me, junkie fuck? This shit's serious!"

Was this really happening? I was in such a deep Heroin hole I thought I might be dreaming. Drew popped up to intercept Thaddaeus and crew before they got too close to the shanty. Thaddaeus was pissed and Drew was making a series of gestures, trying to soothe him. But Thaddaeus would not be appeased.

"That's bullshit, Drew, and you know it. Did you really think you could fuck me?"

Thaddaeus slapped Drew. I think I actually laughed aloud for a split second, because it was that ridiculous, improbable, and unfathomable. Like a sitcom moment. But Drew was calm and strong. He stood his ground.

"You need to chill the fuck out, Thaddaeus."

"Bitch, please."

Thaddaeus slapped him again, and then again. Then, his boys surrounded Drew and held his arms behind his back. Then Thaddaeus started punching Drew in the gut.

Was this really happening?

Drew pulled this WWE move, rearing up, and giving Thaddaeus a double kick to the chest. Everyone broke into a melee. Was this really happening? Then I heard a gunshot. And then I heard another gunshot.

I got to my feet, shaking off every last bit of Heroin haze. I didn't know whose gun it was, or who fired the shots—but Drew was holding it now, and one of Thaddaeus's boys had a hole in his head. The remaining five of us froze as our immediate neighbors made a beeline for the exit.

"You done fucked up now, bitch!" Thaddaeus declared as Drew alternated pointing the gun at him and his two remaining goons.

"Drew," I had a humiliating squeak of a voice. "What's going on?"

"I got this, Sonny. Just grab your gear. We're going."

"How far you think you gonna get, bitch?" asked Thaddaeus.

He didn't answer because he didn't have time to: One of Thaddaeus's boys, the fat one, grabbed Drew by the hair and held a knife to his throat.

I started having an out of body experience, and, as I floated upward, I saw myself spring into action like a football player. I rammed my skull directly into the fat goon's bloated spine. The knife went flying.

"Hold him!" Drew screamed, and I did, but the fucker was over 300 pounds and just rolled over on me. There was another gun shot. And then another.

For moments, it was like there were two of me: My consciousness, detached and ghost-like, floating like an astral projection, and my physical self (which I had no control over) stuck at the bottom of a deadly dogpile. But soon enough, the two abruptly crashed back into one. I was drenched in blood and piss as the fat fuck went limp. Drew rolled him off, pulled me to my feet, and slapped the knife into my hand. We were facing off against Thaddaeus and his only remaining goon.

Unbelievably, Thaddaeus released a triumphant blast of laughter.

"That gun only had four bullets," he informed us as he pulled another one out of his waistband. "But this one right here's got six!"

Drew aimed at Thaddaeus and pulled his trigger: Click.

"Sonny... Run!"

If only Thaddaeus and his gun had been standing behind us, we might have sprinted outside and up an embankment onto a busy street, someplace public where Thaddaeus wouldn't dare kill us. But that wasn't the case. Thaddaeus and his gun, and his one remaining goon, were standing between us and the exit. When Drew suggested we run, there was only one way to go: In. Down. Deep.

The very prospect terrified me, but not as much as an angry Heroin dealer with a gun. So, we ran, side by side, straight into the darkness. I heard two bullets whiz over our heads before a third clipped my ear.

"He shot my fucking ear off, Drew!"

"Keep running!" He grabbed my left hand. "I know where I'm going."

Soon we were beyond the lights of the campfires and burn barrels. At that point, it didn't matter if my eyes were opened or closed, so I let Drew pull me downward like a rag doll. Down into a blackness more complete than anything I'd ever felt.

That might have been months ago, or maybe it's been years. Time moves differently down here. Drew's still with me, though not as good looking as he used to be. It will take a lot more than death to split us up, that's for damn sure! He's been here every step of the way: Down the rabbit hole and through the Nine Circles of Hell. My light and my guide into the Realms of the Old Ones. I never could have made it without him.

I'm exactly where I need to be.

And I'm about to meet God.

CHAPTER TWO

As we scrambled into the darkness, Thaddaeus popped off the rest of his bullets. Luckily, there was no further contact.

"You're dead now!" he called after us. "I'll be back with my dogs!"

Drew was dragging me deeper into the main runoff channel and, soon, down a connecting maintenance corridor. The extreme adrenaline surge that had sucked me prematurely from the Warm Oblivion was fading fast, sending me back into the foggy throes of semi-lucidity. I was like a toddler being pulled through a crowded department store by an impatient parent. The searing pain of my shattered ear turned into a warm throb as the river of blood running down my neck slowed to a trickle. Simultaneously, the whining of a tiny mosquito grew persistently louder until it became a screaming ring against my bruised eardrum.

My mind flashed highlights and low points of the past few minutes: Thaddaeus and his boys. Guns and knives. Chinese guy with a blast wound to the left temple—his chrome grill knocked clean out of his mouth. Had that just happened? Did a fat fucker just die on top of me? How much of this blood was mine, and how much was someone else's? Was Thaddaeus really coming back to kill us?

I might have chosen different thoughts if I'd known I would never see the Moon or the stars again. I might have imagined the Sun rising and setting against the desert sky. I might have imagined meteor showers and lightning storms, eclipses and aurora borealis. One of those super flocks of tiny black birds that swarm and swirl like plumes of smoke. Snow-capped peaks and fighter jets flying in formation. An airplane's eye view of America, a patchwork of green and tan fields broken by rivers and purple mountains majesty. The Ocean, the Ocean, the Ocean.

Instead, it was: Dead bodies in bloody track suits, staring down the barrel of a gun, and Thaddaeus laughing manically.

"Don't pass out on me, Sonny Boy!"

Drew was deftly maneuvering us through a series of passageways, down stairwells, and across open spaces vast as parking lots. We were deeper inside the immense labyrinth than I'd ever been (or cared to go), but it was familiar. I'd heard about its schematics often in Drew's stories. Now, random bits from years of ramblings returned as recollections presented in tightly organized dossiers. Drew narrated with the expert aplomb of a lauded professor. Imagine it over scenes of us twisting and turning, like a voice-over:

"The upper network, where we live, is all municipal: The storm drains, flood channels, maintenance corridors, sewers, gas and electrical conduits. You can get anywhere in the city. Then, beneath the Stratosphere, there's a core structure. It's like a reverse skyscraper underground: Levels upon levels. Some are developed, while others are completely skeletal with rows of concrete pillars but no walls. It's called The Web because there are tunnels leading to other stations, all emanating out from the center like a spider web."

There were obstacles as we ran: Piles of trash and abandoned shopping carts, small but angry congregations of human ghouls passing glass pipes, drunken zombies passed out in puddles of their own piss and vomit. My diaphragm started seizing. My lungs were burning. The muscles in my legs were threatening to detach from the bones. The world around me was fading, but somehow Drew's voice in my head equalized the physical agony.

"There's a secret organization of casino owners, politicians, and bankers called The Forlorn Order who built The Web with funds diverted from secret Government programs. It's an active system trafficked by smugglers, money launderers, and powerful white-collar criminals. Elite lowlifes. The deepest levels were abandoned in the 1990s. No one knows why for certain, but rumors reference riots, death-squads, and a man-made epidemic. It's a jungle, Sonny. There's no rule of law at those depths. Not even unwritten codes. Just chaos."

I must have passed out because I have the faintest recollection of being slung over Drew's shoulder like a sack of dirty laundry before waking up with my head in his lap. He was cleaning and bandaging up my ear.

"Is it still there?" I asked groggily.

"Still there, Sonny Boy. Just a bit smaller now."

Drew and I were situated on a dirty mattress in an abandoned janitor's closet. It was relatively spacious compared to our shack, though significantly putrefied by the less-courteous tenants who came before us. The walls, illuminated by lantern, were drenched in graffiti. There was a utility sink and shelves that organized various soaps, detergents, and solvents, along with the dripping remnants of a thousand dead candles.

"I found this place a few months ago," Drew explained. "It's too far out of the way to be a home base, but I've been using it as a storage locker. We can rest here for a few hours Sonny, but we can't stay long. Thaddaeus..."

Thaddaeus wasn't kidding when he said he'd be back to sic his dogs on us. The fucker was deep into the dogfighting circuit (when he wasn't slinging or running dope) and had access to kennels full of trained attackers. We wouldn't be hard to find since I'd left a trail of blood the entire way.

"Drew," I ventured, "did we really just get in a shoot-out with gangsters?"

"I'll explain everything, Sonny. But first: Let me give you a shot." The offer, even under these unique circumstances, was surprising. Drew and I had shared a lot over the years: Toothbrushes, shit buckets—we even had a threesome with a rebellious Christian missionary who came down to talk with us about Jesus. But drugs were a different story.

When it came to Heroin, it was strictly "to each his own," which is probably why our friendship was so solid. Nothing splits a friendship faster that sharing a stash. But after what I'd just been through, and considering my ear was a hot mess, I was in no position to turn down a free ticket to the Warm Oblivion. Drew skillfully cooked up a couple syringes, tied me up, spiked me, and there it was: Freedom. Then he lit two cigarettes with a single match and placed one between my lips.

His explanation for our deadly clash with Thaddaeus was complex and nebulous. Also, I was bombed. I couldn't have followed a set of train tracks much less an hours-long confessional. He'd pulled some kind of scam, some sort of bait-and-switch that saw Thaddaeus separated from a sizable chunk of his product. There was a supporting cast of characters that included his ex-stepsister (who may or may not be a famous socialite), a hacker up in Canada, a banker in the Caribbean, and a dirty cop up in Reno (all of whom owed Drew "favors"). There was stuff about Bitcoins and cloned websites. Bottom line: It was a swindle. Drew had stolen from Thaddaeus. Making things infinitely more severe, he'd just killed two of the dealer's lieutenants. Drew was a dead man if he ever went back topside—and so was I.

"But Drew, why?"

"I'll tell you everything, Sonny. But first: Let me give you another shot."

Another shot? Unheard of! It was an unabashed attempt to calm my nerves, thereby making me more susceptible and sympathetic to whatever he was about to tell me (sell me?). But I had absolutely no intention of saying "No" to the offer. A few moments later, I felt like a buoy floating on an ocean of Warm Oblivion.

"Do you know what a pilgrim is, Sonny?"

"Of course I know what a pilgrim is, Drew," I thought but didn't say as Drew continued.

"A pilgrim is anyone who goes on a long trek, usually on foot, to a destination of great spiritual significance. Christians considered the act of pilgrimage to be a form of self-imposed exile, where a person learns the truth about the world: Humanity and divinity.

"It's a process of transformation from wretchedness to beatification." His voice was atypically hypnotic. I imagined the two of us sitting on the crest of a massive sand dune at twilight, looking down on the full expanse of Death Valley and all the way to the Pacific Ocean. "It's time for us to take a pilgrimage Sonny. It's time for us to transform."

"What? Where?"

"A place I've been dreaming about all my life, Sonny. A beautiful place somewhere inside the Earth itself. A sacred place. It's like, I've always had this subconscious echo of it down in my reptile brainstem. You could hear it too, Sonny, if you listened hard enough. And Las Vegas, or the desert it's built on, it just so happens to be one of only six portals on the entire planet that can take us there."

Drew pulled a rectangle of paper out of his pocket and unfolded it. It was a hand-drawn map, and he'd point at different areas as he spoke:

"Below The Forlorn Order's Web there's a system called Wonderland. It began as a joint project between the US Government and the Freemasons at the end of World War II. Stewardship was given to FEMA in 1978. Wonderland connects every major US city with corridors as far north as Alaska and south down to Nazca. If there's a conspiracy involving a shadow government and a race of aliens called The Grays, all the answers will be found in Wonderland."

It was hard to take in at first. Hard because it implied that my best friend Drew was insane. Like, how could he possibly believe this? But one thing about Drew, his enthusiasm is infectious. Always has been. What he was saying was unbelievable, but I wanted to believe it because he believed it. And when you're as high as I was, it was fun to believe it—easy if you just let yourself.

Like this one time, in college, when my friends and I dressed up as KISS for Halloween. We got so high and so into character that, for a few hours, I thought we really were KISS, and I was Peter Criss. And I loved my bandmates like brothers, and I couldn't wait to go on tour with them in support of *Love Gun* and *Destroyer*.

Now, years later, with Drew in a room underground, I let myself remember clips from *Time Bandits* and *The Goonies*. And so, I let myself go a little bit crazy. And I liked it.

"Even if it doesn't exist, that's okay because Wonderland is just as stop along the way. We're going so deep, Sonny, there isn't even a word for it yet—except maybe Xanadu or Shangri-La.

"I've always imagined caves coated in luminescent algae that open onto expanses vaster than Montana. Fields of nutritious fauna and fresh-water lakes full of fishes. Even meat from herds of moles the size of buffalo. If there are intelligent societies (which I'm assuming there will be), they'll have figured out how to harness the Earth's thermal energy. There's enough power beneath us to light up a million Las Vegases."

"And you know how to get there?" I inquired.

"Not exactly," he told me, but he knew where to find a guy named Archibald: "He's a Utopist, with an entire community of free-loving hippies. They've been down here since the 1980s. He knows the way."

"And you really think we'll eventually get to... Xanadu?"

"I know we can. I've been planning this for years. Studying and stockpiling. I was just waiting for the perfect time to set out, Sonny. The perfect time and the perfect partner."

"Me? How can I possibly be the perfect partner, Drew?" I'd never held myself in particularly high esteem.

"From the moment I met you Sonny, I knew you were special. I feel a mystical connection with you, like we've traveled together in previous lifetimes. We might have been Lewis and Clark, or crew members on a tramp steamer sailing down the Congo. You feel it too, don't you Sonny? It's like, Destiny."

I found myself crying. It was a mixture of genuine joy and nauseating terror.

"I didn't plan to start out by running for our lives, but this big score was the final piece of the puzzle. We'll need it, Sonny."

He was right. Without a sizable stash to sustain us on a journey (any journey), we'd probably die from detoxification sickness within a few days. For Drew, addiction was the anchor keeping him chained to the surface, the only thing preventing him from pursuing his life's ambition, bizarre and improbable as it may be. The same was true for me too. I hardly relished the idea of descending into a claustrophobic underworld, but I'd given up on humanity years ago. There was nothing left for me topside besides Drew and Heroin.

"How long does the pilgrimage last?" I inquired.

"Eighteen days."

"Eighteen days? That's a long time!"

"At least eighteen days. Let me explain."

"There's an Amazonian tribe that protects one of the other portals, one that's hidden beneath Aztec ruins. Every few years, Shamans go on underground vision quests, and it takes them eighteen days to get someplace they call The Land of Ancestors. It's a city populated by benevolent giants. So, I figure it will take us at least that long, too."

"What about when we run out of Heroin, though?"

"We won't need it anymore. By then, we'll have something even better. No more pain—ever. I promise."

Now, I've never been a sucker. I don't put much stock in big dreams or fast talkers. But who wouldn't want to buy what he was selling?

"What do you say, Sonny? Will you be my Pilgrim Pal?"

If he was trying to find Xanadu and wanted me to come along, then so be it. Even then, though, at my most committed to his insanity, I didn't honestly consider I might never breathe outside air again.

One thing that gave me pause, though, I'd never seen Drew kill anyone before. And now, the images were burned in my brain. He hadn't hesitated, he never lost his cool. He made it look easy. And that made me very uneasy. Like, maybe he'd done it before—and was good at it. But I loved him.

"Yeah, Drew. I'm with you."

He hugged me so tight all my uncertainties melted away—for a little while at least. "You won't regret this, Sonny Boy!" We celebrated with a third shot of Heroin before I slept like a baby, without a care in the world—like a fetus in a womb of Warm Oblivion, breathing embryonic ambrosia.

We woke up to the sound of barking dogs coming through the air ducts. "They're getting close, Sonny. Come on. Get naked."

We threw our clothes in a pile and huddled around a deep utility sink in the corner. There was no running water, but Drew emptied a murky bucket of rainwater into it. Then he grabbed a canister of Comet.

"Scrub down."

Drew and I had always been semi-attentive to our personal hygiene. Ahead of the curve, at least. We always made certain to wash our armpits, dicks, and assholes at least once a day. But this wasn't some whore's bath: This was some industrial strength deep-cleaning.

My ear stung like hell when detergent hit my wound.

"Don't get any of that shit in your eyes, Sonny."

After a rinse and rubdown, we tossed our clothes into the sink along with a fresh bucket of murky water. Drew emptied an entire bottle of bleach on everything. Our wardrobes were then rinsed in another murky bucket and wrung out before we re-dressed.

"That should throw the dogs off our scent for a while, but it won't be enough." Drew drenched a couple dirty towels in gasoline poured from a rusty can. "We'll wear these around our heads."

Drew was much more prepared for our pilgrimage than I could have possibly realized. Over the past few weeks, he'd assembled two backpacks, "Pilgrim Packs" he called them, each containing a few dozen needles, spoons, a 12 pack of lighters, a big box of waterproof strike-anywhere wooden matches, a carton of smokes, a handful of glow sticks, a ball of string, a roll of aluminum foil, a couple single-battery flashlights, candles, a two-pound bag of beef jerky, toilet paper, a water purification kit, a utility knife, and an assortment of hard candies. The only significant difference between our packs was that Drew's bag had a fist-sized chunk of Heroin and an empty gun in it.

"We can't use flashlights yet, Sonny. That'll lead them right to us." He pulled a set of high-tech black goggles from a box and put them on. "I could only afford one set of night-vision headgear, so I'll lead the way." He tied a length of rope around my waist. "This'll make sure we don't get separated. Hey, don't look so worried, Sonny. You trust me, right?"

Based on the events of the past 12 hours, there was absolutely no reason I should have trusted Drew. But he was my best and only friend. More than that, he was my Pilgrim Pal from past lives. I'd follow him anywhere, even if it meant dying along the way. We were tighter than KISS in 1976.

"I trust you, Drew."

And then we were off on the ride of our lifetimes.

We crept out of the closet, heads wrapped like jihadists, and off into the darkness. The gas fumes burned my eyes and nasal cavity, but the pain came with its own, not completely unpleasant, intoxication. At first, I kept my hands on Drew's shoulders, but before long, I dropped back and clung exclusively to the umbilicus between us.

The echoing cries of barking dogs were closing in before abruptly fading into the gray area behind us. The labyrinth was occasionally lit by flickering yellow bulbs. But most often, everything was pitch black. It wasn't long before my mind began to conjure strange blobs of colors, like when you rub your eyes for a while. Then, I was seeing a myriad of faces materializing all around me, abstract but clear, like seeing shapes in clouds. The echoes of barking dogs continued to fade until they were only barely detectable.

"We'll get to the Web in an hour, Sonny." It was another twisting, sweaty, grueling whirl through tunnels, hallways, and stairwells. Eventually, we arrived at the opening of a wide, sharply curving ramp.

"There used to be a fleet of golf carts to usher people down to the Staging Chamber, but we don't have access to anything so luxurious." Drew untied the rope around my waist, picked out a couple shopping carts littering the immediate vicinity, and tied them together.

"Hop in!"

"What, we're riding down in shopping carts?"

"We could walk, but the ramp spirals more than seventy levels down."

"Yeah, but that sounds pretty dangerous."

Drew laughed. He laughed so sincerely it wasn't long before I was laughing right along with him. "Come on Sonny, live a little! Besides, the sooner we get to the Staging Chamber, the sooner we can set-up camp and get high."

As we raced in rickety metal cages into a corkscrew of darkness, it first occurred to me that I might be having the best day of my life. It was certainly better than any other day I could easily recall. Mere hours after being involved in multiple murders and suffering personal physical disfigurement, I was blasting noisily through the gloom, Drew hooting and hollering from the cart in front of me, where he maneuvered us by wedging a broomstick against the back wheels.

"We're on a Highway to Hell, Sonny Boy! Going down!"

It was wide smiles and gut-slapping laughter all the way, dizzy on fumes and centrifugal force. We were nearing speeds that might have simulated weightlessness.

Eventually, we spilled out into a vast, flat expanse. Our train wobbled and shook violently before spilling us out onto dusty concrete. The cages continued to slide, eventually crashing into the base of a virtual mountain of shopping carts. It was a visual record of the intrepid explorers who came before us. Other pilgrims perhaps.

A hard landing to say the least, but even a bloody nose and some cracked teeth couldn't dampen my mood. Drew hurried to his feet, pulled me to mine, and gave me a bear-hug.

The Staging Chamber was an immense domed enclosure, at least the size of an Olympic sports arena. It was faintly lit by a single overcast beam that shown down from the apex.

"It's refractory technology, Sonny," Drew told me. "They bounce that light down from the surface on a series of solar cells and mirrors. It was designed to keep construction workers and contractors from losing track of time." Drew explained how he'd only been down to

The Staging Chamber once before, about six months ago. After an arduous, exhausting, six-hour return trek back up the ramp, he knew he wouldn't be back again until the official start of his pilgrimage, our pilgrimage, this pilgrimage.

Besides the mountain of shopping carts, the far end of the chamber was littered with massive mounds of construction debris. Chunks of cracked concrete, twisted girders, even a few dead tractors. There was an immense crane, something you'd expect to see loading containers onto cargo ships, standing like a skeletonized dinosaur in the midst of it all, like a monster trapped in an opaque snow globe.

"This is the top level of The Web," Drew explained. "This is where all the raw materials were loaded in and where larger components were fabricated. Behind that pile of wreckage back there are some huge freight elevators. That's our way down. They don't run anymore, so we'll be climbing down one of the shafts."

What little refracted light that remained was fading, so we made haste setting up camp a few yards down from the ramp. Drew figured we'd be safest for the night if we stayed close to the wall, "even if some nasty Web heads catch wind of us." Once the fire was lit, he cooked up a couple extra tasty shots of Lady H and sent me off into the Warm Oblivion, head resting on my Pilgrim Pack like a pillow.

"Hey Sonny, what do you know about Hollow Earth theory?"

"Do tell, Drew."

"It's mostly bullshit, especially that stuff about an inner sun and reverse gravity. But the truth is, scientists know almost nothing about the planet's consistency. The farthest we've drilled is eight miles down, and that's just a hole the size of a coffee can. The guy who discovered Halley's Comet, smart guy, he thought there are actually three concentric Earths, and we're on the top layer. Each one has oceans and a breathable atmosphere capable of sustaining life. And each one has its own rotation, and that explains why the magnetic Poles are always wobbling..." The campfire settled into a pile of embers.

"Where do you learn all this stuff, Drew?"

"Library, Sonny."

"You read all of this stuff at the library?"

"No, I got to the library and I watch a lot of videos on YouTube."

I started having strange dreams that weren't exactly nightmares, but weren't especially pleasant, either. I dreamed of sailing across a Lake of Fire and ripping my own flesh from my chest. I dreamed of staring into the eyes of the World Maggot and summoning up a necromancer. I felt an ancient rumbling miles beneath me, something with an overwhelming enormity that made me utterly microscopic in comparison. Then an earthquake of anarchy erupted, and Drew was screaming: "Run, Sonny, Run!"

Except I wasn't dreaming anymore—and there was pain.

"Run, Sonny, Run!"

I scrambled into my Pilgrim Pack for a glow-stick and I cracked it. As I got to my feet, the noxious green illumination revealed an atmosphere thick with bats. They were swirling and dive-bombing, slapping my face with their wings, clawing and biting.

Worse, the ground was swarming with roaches, biggest I'd ever seen. Some were the size of bars of soap. Many found their way inside my pant legs where their feet stung like needles as they charted courses towards my crotch. A herd of albino rats the size of rabbits rumbled past. Someone, or something, was tootling in the deeper darkness, laughing. Somewhere, dogs were barking.

"Run, Sonny! Run!"

Drew was being mauled by a monster, a vicious, hideous codger with a disgusting beard, sharp black teeth, and long thick fingernails like yellow daggers. Its soulless eyes were covered by a semi-transparent membrane. Drew was fighting for his life, and he was obviously losing.

"Run! Run! Run!"

CHAPTER
THREE

"OPEN YOUR EYES."

I opened my eyes and saw Drew standing over me. The Sun was shining behind his head giving him a spikey, radiant halo.

"We made it, Sonny Boy." I was lying on warm concrete just outside the mouth of our home tunnel. Drew had saved my life. He must have dragged me out while I was unconscious.

I heard a buzzing. Drew pointed into the azure sky at a two-seater aircraft cruising in the distance. "Rear Admiral Richard E. Byrd was an ace combat pilot in the first World War and a national hero," Drew explained. "In 1926 he set out to be the first person to fly over the North Pole—but ended up somewhere else entirely."

"Where?" I asked

"Where do you think, Sonny?" Drew's face started turning pink then red. Beads of sweat ran down his face.

"Xanadu? Shangri-La?" My hands hurt.

"Agartha." There was blood on Drew's teeth and in his mouth.

"Tell me the story, Drew." My ribs hurt. It was hard to breathe. The back of my head was throbbing.

"Can't right now, Sonny," he said as his face began to contort and distort.

"Why?" I asked, as my stomach dropped.

"Because you're waking up."

The sweat streaming off Drew's face turned to blood. The Sun went black and the ground beneath me crumbled, sending me somersaulting into oppressive nothingness. Disembodied laughter taunted me and intimidated me. Dogs were barking. I remembered everything as my body crash landed with a bone-crushing thud.

I convulsed in a double earthquake of physical agony and emotional ruin. It was a shattering of the senses that was momentarily transcendent, until I returned to my mortal coil only to find the landscape decimated, my soul eviscerated, my core obliterated. I wished I could, and I tried in vain to reclaim my unconsciousness, a chance to reunite with Drew once more.

A primal, guttural utterance forced its way from my diaphragm and through my shredded vocal cords, erupting with the urgent intensity of an air raid siren.

"How could you?" I asked myself, "How could you leave him, you pathetic coward?"

"It's not your fault, Sonny," said Drew's voice in my head. I knew I was just imagining what I hoped he'd say, but I pretended anyway, like he was speaking to me telepathically from someplace not too far away.

"I left you! I'm the worst friend in the world!"

"I was already dead. Remember?"

The vicious, hideous codger must have crept up on us in the Staging Chamber sometime after the fire had died down, and we had long gone silent. I don't know why it chose to pounce on Drew instead of me, but by the time I was awake and on my feet (in the vortex of a perfect storm of bats, bugs, and albino rats) it was already too late.

The he-crone clung to Drew's back like a rabid chimpanzee before taking him down. It bit into Drew's neck and pulled away with a mouthful of meat and sinew. It dug its claws under Drew's ribcage. I could see bone, burgundy liver, and gushing blood. Frenzied bats swarmed as roaches, some big as the palm of my hand, crawled inside Drew's deepest wounds. The codger began screaming like a wild boar enjoying an orgasm of bloodlust.

"Run, Sonny! Run!" With a free arm and the last of his strength, Drew lobbed something in my direction: The night-vision goggles.

"It's killing you, Drew!"

"Run, Sonny! Run!"

God forgive me: I abandoned my best friend, my soul brother from past lives. I strapped on the goggles, and I ran. I ran with the roaches and the gargantuan white rats and other scurrying lifeforms I can't identify even now.

I ran straight towards the mountain of wreckage at the far side of the dome. The codger's squeal echoed throughout the chamber, until another call (slightly higher pitched) chimed in from a distance. And then a third. There were others. The codger was inviting its sinister brethren to the feast. I heard a fourth blood-curdling squeal, and a fifth. I looked up and saw figures climbing down from the cab of the monstrous crane, grappling and swinging from the upper tiers like evil, infected acrobats. They were everywhere.

As I climbed over boulders of concrete and tetanus-infested rebar, I could feel and see arms reaching up for me from between the cracks, clawing at my ankles. There were more of them living in the crevasses beneath me! I could hear them hissing!

I never would have made it through and over those jagged crumbles, the twisted scaffolding and the mechanical debris, without the goggles. But I made it. Scraped and bleeding, bat bitten with stinging cockroaches in my briefs, retching from fear and already suffering an intensity of guilt I never knew existed—but I made it.

I faced four huge openings to what had been four immense freight elevators. The lifts had long been decommissioned and dismantled. Only four vast shafts remained, each a potentially bottomless pit.

I chose the second one from the right for my descent, a decision I made instantly and instinctually as if the other three weren't actually viable options at all. I spotted an access ladder just an easy step from the perilous lip. I leaned forward and gripped the upper rung tightly, but as my feet followed, a shock went through my system.

Some fucker had welded razor blades to the top handhold. The tendons in my palms were instantly severed and all my fingers went limp. All sounds were muted except my own heartbeat as gravity pulled me backwards in slow motion.

I assumed this was my swan song and, truth be told, that suited me fine. No more pain and no more guilt. At one point during my turbulent tumble, I hit a net that had been strung across the shaft. I have no idea if it was meant as a safety precaution or a trap, but it didn't matter: The fibers were so rotted, it barely slowed me down before I snapped right through it.

But even my eventual landing hadn't killed me. It was just a momentary detour into the comparative Heaven of unconsciousness. Now, as I continued to emerge from the fog, there wasn't anything I wanted more than to claw my way back into that emptiness.

I was viciously dope sick.

I'd been "taken in", to put it non-confrontationally, by Meister Hauptnadel (whose name I can't even write without wincing), an egomaniacal German psychonaut who sounded like your stereotypical mad scientist.

"Vee fount you in a pile off mut. You hat fallen... so very far."

He sounded exactly like Dr. Heiter (played by Dieter Laser) in *The Human Centipede*, I remember thinking.

I'd been pulled from a pit of semisoft clay and cleansed, he explained. But any sense of gratitude I might have felt was stifled by the realization I was strapped on an operating table, arms outstretched lethal-injection style, wrists bound.

"You haff been aschleep for quite some time. Many off your bone's vill... never be zee same."

I was covered in a stained white sheet that hid the feeding tube in my stomach and the catheter in my dick. My hands had been crudely stitched and wrapped but my fingers were still useless. There were several bright lamps pointed at my face, making it impossible to see beyond my immediate surroundings.

Hauptnadel looked like a Cenobite.

"Sank you for zee lenses. Zey haff given me some... very interestink insights." He was talking about Drew's night-vision goggles which he now wore proudly has part of his own ensemble. It was somehow the least bizarre aspects of his attire.

He sported sets of mechanical "fingers" attached over the tops of his hands. Each one, including the thumbs, was capped in a thick metal syringe, and each needle's thick tip dripped a different colored fluid.

He had five more metal syringes implanted, needle-first, in a horizontal line across his forehead like a crown. He wore a white lab coat over what looked like a shredded latex bodysuit. Bits of machinery, gears, and stray wires pushed through the tears, hinting at possible cybernetic enhancements.

Hauptnadel presided over a dozen Acolytes of Ascension who were all female, transgender, or extremely androgynous. Most displayed shocking modifications, including artificial horns, extensive facial and eyeball tattoos, stretched lips, nostrils and ears. They had implants made from wood, bone, and a gamut of metal alloys. Some of them even had their mouths or eyes sewn shut. The only thing they all had in common was a silver plug in the center of their foreheads.

"Haff you ever hurt off trepannink?" Hauptnadel asked me, once he was certain I was cognizant enough to understand him.

Trepanning, he explained, "is zee practice off removink a section of bone from zee skull. Zis is done to increase blood flow to zee brain. Zee benefits are... outstandink!"

He spoke in platitudes, often pausing for dramatic effect, curling his lips for exaggerated emphasis.

"Every vone of zem, mein Acolytes," he would beam with pride, "has achievft levels of consciousness expansion you cannot yet fazom... Zough perhaps, someday, you vill."

To demonstrate, Hauptnadel had his Apex Acolyte, his favorite, kneel down before him. Then he removed the plug in her forehead. Pink tissue throbbed intently, like a piece of glistening meat was trying to break free from her head and escape.

Hauptnadel reviewed the needles on his fingers, explaining, "Different compounds haff different effects... but all of zem push boundaries you nefer knew existed."

He pushed a needle deep inside his Acolyte's skull, between her hemispheres, where it deposited an appropriate dosage directly into her pituitary gland.

"Soon, she vill begin speakink in prehistoric and mystical lankuages."

In place of the plug, Hauptnadel inserted a glass globe that allowed her brain to continue pulsating as blood and other fluids accumulated and sloshed inside it. Her eyes rolled back in her head and she did, indeed, speak "languages" I'd never heard before (punctuated by long periods of shrieking) for hours.

Hauptnadel played ear-slashing electro-tribal music, dancing, and gloating.

"You see? Do you see? She is ascendink!"

When her spasms finally subsided, the globe was removed and her plug reinserted into her forehead.

He could work himself into similar frenzies by modifying and pushing the syringes permanently mounted into his forehead, constantly adjusting an ever-flowing combination of potions and tinctures streaming into his brain, like an audio technician dialing in the sonic sweet spot.

"Can you help me?" I implored, when my voice finally returned. "Do you have Heroin?" I was dripping with sweat, periodically convulsing, and covered in my own vomit.

"Oh yes, mein younk cadet. Vee indulge all fancies here," he teased. "In fact, vone of zees has exactly vhat you seek." He fanned his needle-fingers and placed one hand in front of the other, creating what looked like a dangerous peacock shadow puppet.

"Can I have it? Please, I'm begging!"

"No no no, mein cadet. You don't haff to beg. You merely haff to choose."

One of his finger syringes, he explained, was filled with an exquisite dose of China White, a junkie's wet dream. The others, he cautioned, could have beautiful or disastrous effects if injected.

"Vone iss LSD und vone iss MDMA. Seferal are research chemicals. Vone iss antifreeze, anozer iss ammonia. So, vich vone vill it be?"

The fact that each syringe was metal made it impossible to judge its contents by color or consistency. Still, for a 10% chance of finding a ticket into the Warm Oblivion, I was willing to risk it all.

"Right hand... middle finger."

Hauptnadel injected liquid deep inside my femoral artery.

This is how I spent my hours, days, even weeks with The Acolytes of Ascension. Most often, whatever Hauptnadel injected me with only exacerbated my agonies. Even when I was certain I hit the MDMA, it couldn't erase the pain in my bones or the sorrow in my heart.

"There's nothing like the real thing, Baby..." I'd hum, pitiful tears dribbling.

When I did finally hit the China White ("Left hand...thumb."), yes, it was glorious.

"Wait, wait, wait," I exclaimed, giggling and drooling. "This reminds me of a scene from *A Nightmare on Elm Street Part 3*!"

Falling back into the Warm Oblivion was like returning home to a lover after a long and bloody war. I wept with joy. Ultimately, however, the vacation from misery only made returning to torture exponentially devastating. Afterwards, I felt like a premature baby dumped out of its incubator onto a cold, filthy floor. Once the China White was discovered and consumed, another shot was loaded and reshuffled. The daily rituals of symphonic, systematic inflictions continued.

I came to understand, much to Hauptnadel's delight, that pain can't be rated on a simple scale of one through ten. It's a vast and infinitely more nuanced spectrum. After experiencing brutal extremes, lesser assaults felt like pleasure. Being bitten, pierced, sliced, even branded became a welcome pleasure (though ever tainted by my all-encompassing dope sickness).

As I'd writhe, Hauptnadel would invite his Acolytes in to observe and participate. "You see, mein beauties? You see how exquisite iss his sufferink?"

He eventually introduced me to Sybil, an Acolyte with her eyes and mouth sewn shut. Her nose was grossly distended into a single, gaping nostril that emitted a slurping noise with every inhalation, a farting noise with each exhalation. Hauptnadel dragged her around by a thick black braid extending from the top of her head.

"Sybil iss psychic," the madman told me. "Vonce vee took her eyes und her tongue, she learnt to decipher riddles und premonitions by zee sense off schmell exclusifely."

Hauptnadel removed her plug, injected her with a finger, and inserted a glass globe. "She eats trough her nose, she fucks trough her nose..." he told me, thrusting his hips to emphasize the F-word. He pulled her onto my torture table. "...Vhich is vie I hat to remoof her scheptum."

Sybil, whose ears were intact, nodded and snorted in agreement. He pulled the sheet away from my emaciated body.

"Now let's see vhat she can tell me about you!"

He shoved Sybil's head between my legs where she feverishly sniffed my testicles, like a pig rooting around for a truffle. After a few moments, she reached out to Hauptnadel, who handed her some chalk and a piece of slate. "Oh, zis iss not goot," he bemoaned as he revealed Sybil's scrawl:

"He's a coward!"

I was one of several cadets, I was told, each housed in a private Conversion Room, being vetted for membership. If selected (and if I survived the indoctrination period), I'd be invited to join the Acolytes, allowed to participate in communal acts of consciousness expansion in a glorious temple adorned in red-velvet with satin-covered mattresses on an impressive altar.

I'd be fitted with permanent stainless-steel rings through my shoulders, ass cheeks, and calves so I could sleep with the other Acolytes: Suspended by hooks over a pit of smoldering coals. I'd be put on a heavy diet of female hormones. And, most importantly, I'd be given a Baptism by Trepanning.

"Zis is just a taste of vhat avaits you," he told me one day before carving a hole into my forehead with a dental drill. I could smell my skull burning as the tiny bore pushed forwards. It broke through with a pop that startled me, followed by the roaring gush of a waterfall.

"Zere, isn't zat nice?" he asked as blood trickled into my eyes, mixing with remnants of a million tears.

"You can join us, mein younk cadet. Vee haff carved out a lofely corner of Hell for ourschelfes." He leaned in and whispered into my ear (the good one): "Vee... haff... Her-r-r-o-in..." rolling his r's, seductively. Every hair on my body stood on end. "Just giff me permission... to open up your Third Eye..." In other words: Submit to trepanning. "But for now, you must choose a finger!"

"Right hand... Index..."

"You've got to get out of here, Sonny," Drew told me after Hauptnadel injected me with a mega-dose of LSD. In my feverish, disembodied state, our two-consciousness aligned on a cosmic level, (or, more likely, in my imagination). Whatever the case, I hung on his every word:

"Everyone here's a slave, Sonny. Hauptnadel's the worst kind of hedonistic hypocrite. He's a fucking poser. Do not let him drill into your head again, Sonny! Do you hear me?"

"How can I get away, Drew?"

"He likes you because you entertain him. Stop playing his games and he'll lose interest. If you're lucky, he'll let you go."

"How am I 'playing his games'? I can barely move."

"Every time you scream, or plead, or cry—you're just feeding his ego. Soon, you'll be begging him to crack your melon and sew your lips shut."

"Tell me what to do, Drew."

Drew explained that Hauptnadel was actually Reginald E. Carmichael, age 35—and he wasn't even German. He came from old steel industry money but, more importantly, his father was a key member of both The Bilderberg Group and The Forlorn Order, giving him access to certain elite areas of The Web. He'd established

The Acolytes of Ascension (with his trust fund) as a way of delving into body modification and experimental drug use while building his personal harem.

"Don't do anything, Sonny. Stop picking fingers and letting his bitches nose-fuck you. When he comes to play, you just dive down deep inside your mind. If you dive down deep enough, I'll be there waiting for you."

It was easier said than done, but well worth the rewards. Giving in to the ravages of pain was essential, I learned, as efforts to suppress Hauptnadel's cruelties only intensified my anguish and his pleasure. Eventually, I was able to dive down deep enough in my mind to connect with Drew on a regular basis, on an astral plane, or at the crossroads of insanity.

"Maybe this is all a dream, Sonny." It was a nice thought to get lost in. "Some tribes believed the Dream World is reality, and everything we perceive to be real is just an illusion," Drew would postulate. "Maybe you're unconscious at the bottom of the elevator shaft. Maybe you're in a coma and your body's trying to heal itself. Sonny, what if this is your *Jacob's Ladder*?"

Day after day, I resisted dope sickness and Hauptnadel's meddling, diving past chasms of psychedelic bliss and blistering psychosis to connect with my mentor at my center.

"Hey Sonny, did I ever tell you about The Thule Society?" Drew asked.

He had, but I didn't interrupt him:

"They were a group of German occultists who formed after World War I and, eventually, they became major players in the Nazi Party. When Hitler realized he was losing World War II, they told him about an ancient city, deep inside the Earth, where the original Aryan race would welcome him as a God. Hitler was so desperate to find it, he sent expeditions to Jerusalem and Antarctica and a bunch of other places, looking for a way to get in..."

Drew's plan for my escape eventually paid off.

"I'ff grown veary off zis vone," I heard Hauptnadel pining to his Apex. "I zought he had potential, but lately, I'm sinkink... not so much. He just lies zere."

"What shall we do with him Master? Feed him to the C.H.U.D.s?"

"Perhaps I vill sell him to zee Creature Pimp. Pull his teeth out and put him to vork in zee glory holes. Or perhaps I vill sell him to zee Skin Traders, or zee Organ Butchers, or zee Sport Hunters..."

"Archibald," I whispered, remembering the name Drew had mentioned in his utility closet hideaway.

"Vhat did he say?"

"Archibald," I croaked a little bit louder.

"He said 'Archibald,' Master," his Apex responded.

"You vant us to take you to Archibald?" Hauptnadel exclaimed with inflated amusement before bursting into maniacal laughter. "He vants us to take him to Archibald!" he repeated, sending his Acolyte into a fit of cackling glee. "You sink I'm such a demon?" Hauptnadel erupted, suddenly appearing legitimately insulted. The Acolyte fell silent. "You sink zere are better opportunities for you down here? Down zere? No no no, you could do much vorse zan endink up unter mein tutelage, younk cadet!" He said those last two words with such venom and contempt it sounded like he was hocking up phlegm.

After enduring all Hauptnadel's batteries, it seemed I'd finally touched one of his nerves. "Take the fucker to The Boatman," he barked at his Apex, completely dropping his fake German accent, exposing his true New Jersey roots. "If he can pay the toll, let him go live with Archibald and the rest of his computer-fuckers! Get him out of here!"

The Acolytes dumped me off the table (the space that had been my entire world for the length of my captivity) onto the frigid floor. They practically yanked the tubes out of my stomach and my dick before wrapping me in a bloody towel and tossing me, naked, into a wheelchair. They pushed me past several rooms, each containing another cadet, before we arrived in a large antechamber with red walls, a brilliant crystal chandelier, and a massive metal door. One of them pulled a lever and the door swung open with the heavy, intentional clunk of a bank vault.

I was ushered down corridors unlike anything I'd seen in the upper labyrinth. They were huge and circular, arced as opposed to straight and angular. There was no graffiti, but I saw numbers periodically scrawled on the walls. Coordinates maybe.

"It's too bad, really," the Acolyte pushing me scolded. "We party hard here. We have good times. Hauptnadel's not perfect, but Archibald's on a whole other trip. They don't party like we do."

It felt like there was sand grinding into the cracked bones in my pelvis, knees, and elbows. It was excruciating. This fact, combined with my obvious weight loss and muscle atrophy, had me wondering if I'd ever walk again.

We met The Boatman at the edge of what turned out to be a vast sewage desalinization tank. He demanded two of my fingernails and a tooth for passage across this lake of shit.

"No smoking!" the hooded Boatman with a braided beard and tattooed hands warned me. "Methane: One spark and, BOOM!"

I hadn't had a cigarette in God knows how long. As he yanked his payment away with plyers, I thought about those wonderful Pilgrim Packs, filled with glorious bounty, no doubt looted and consumed by the fiends infesting the Staging Chamber long ago.

The vessel was nothing but a decomposing wooden platform balanced over eight floating innertubes. The Acolytes heaved me aboard without an ounce of finesse before retreating hastily from the stench and fumes, scurrying home to their Master.

The Boatman used a pole to propel us forward, lifting and plunging it into the disgusting depths. We hadn't gone far before I realized his hands weren't tattooed. They were stained with shit from ferrying God-knows-how-many passengers along this vile expanse.

"Haven't taken anyone to Archibald's in a long time," he informed me, but was otherwise silent.

Our voyage was occasionally illuminated by bursting clouds of blue gas, each with the potential to set off a catastrophic chain reaction.

But I wasn't worried. As we approached our destination, I was elated to see Drew standing on the shore, waving us over. He was covered in blood, missing his left eye, and his guts were hanging out, but he seemed happy as a kid on Christmas. "You made it Sonny!"

"We made it, Drew."

"Who's Drew?" asked The Boatman.

Soon, I was lying in front of a massive iron doorway, imposing and ornate.

There was an inscription: "Children of the Inferno" and below that, "We Welcome Those with No Hope Left to Abandon."

Drew rang the doorbell. His mutilated specter was giddy.

CHAPTER
FOUR

FOR ME, BEING IN a medically induced coma was like being trapped in a haunted house.

I wanted to wake up but couldn't. I could part the curtains and detect a sunlit world outside, but all the doors and windows were locked and the glass was unbreakable. And as opposed to the timeless nature of cold unconsciousness or the Warm Oblivion, every second dragged like Purgatory. Every minute was a decade and every hour an eternity.

Chemically imprisoned, this house of horrors became another labyrinth: Impossibly large with dozens of stories, connected by rickety staircases and catwalks. Each level was an intricate series of dimly lit, rat infested hallways teeming with all manner of Minotaur.

I'd seek shelter but only nerve-shredding terror lay behind every door: Evil clowns, creepy kids, screaming phantoms, sadistic surgeons, skinless sinners. There were Satanic blood rituals, human centipedes, decomposing corpses, torture chambers, vomit orgies, and chainsaw massacres. I saw things that made me want to gouge my eyes out.

I was always on the run. I could hear dogs barking and Thaddaeus closing in on me: "Give me back my Heroin, bitch!" If I was lucky enough to give him the slip, Hauptnadel and his Acolytes awaited to stab at me with poison needles or grab at my dick. Vicious, hideous codgers crawled on all fours across floors, walls, and ceilings, unencumbered by the laws of gravity. The Boatman wanted to pull out the rest of my teeth with his shitty fingers.

Thankfully, I found Drew. We sealed ourselves in the attic, built a blanket fort, and holed-up inside like kids with flashlights. He calmed me down and passed the time by retelling me many of my favorite stories.

"Hey Sonny, did I ever tell you about the Green Children of Woolpit?"

"I think you did but go ahead and tell me again."

"They appeared in Eastern England in the 12th Century. The town was actually called Wolf Pit because there were a bunch of deep holes to trap wolves that would otherwise eat the livestock. Well, what comes crawling out of a pit one day, but two children. A brother and a sister. They spoke an unknown language and wore strange clothes, but most bizarre: They had green skin. The younger one, the brother got sick and died, but the girl thrived. She was taken in by a local nobleman who named her Agnes and taught her English. After a few years, she was finally able to tell everyone where she and her brother came from."

I pictured it in my mind.

"She described land of perpetual twilight; an underground city called Saint Martin's Land where everyone had green skin. Agnes said she and her brother were tending their father's flock when they decided to follow the sound of tolling bells through a series of tunnels and caves. They were lost for days before finally emerging from the wolf pit, where they felt sunshine on their skin for the very first time. Eventually, Agnes lost her green hue and lived the rest of her days in Woolpit—where she gained a reputation for being quite the slut. Underground people like to get freaky."

I had no memory of anything beyond arriving at the iron doorway, but Drew filled me in on the basics:

They reset a few of my bones and surgically bolted my pelvis back together. They grafted extra tendons from my calves into my hands, so I'd be able to move my fingers again. They cleared some intestinal blockage and cured a yeast infection in my urethra. They even fixed my teeth with implants and did the best they could to rebuild my mangled ear.

"You were almost dead, Sonny," Drew explained. "They didn't think you'd be able to survive the shock of multiple surgeries."

"How long will we be stuck in here?" I pondered. "Drew, I think it's been a lot longer than 18 days."

"Don't worry about it. Hey, did I ever tell you about the Icosaméron? It's a twelve-hundred-page book written by Giacomo Casanova in 1788. It's about an underground utopian city called Mégamicres populated by a race of multicolored, hermaphroditic dwarves..."

Eventually, the windows of my haunted house began to open. Rays of light penetrated the darkest corners, banishing all abominable apparitions.

"You'll be coming out soon, Sonny. I'm going to scout up ahead. Your job is to meet with Archibald and find out how to get past Wonderland. Now pay attention to the female doctor."

I was in a hospital bed and Drew was gone.

She told me her name was Dr. Sasha. She handed me a Polaroid and asked: "Do you know who this is?"

I was looking at an emaciated, Gollum-esque creature on a gurney. Its eyes were sunken and black. Its dried lips receded into an O revealing a ghastly, skeleton's smile full of cracked shards of teeth. It was naked except for a towel covering its crotch and caked in filth. It reminded me of those alien autopsy photos that were popular in the 1990s.

"Is it... a prop from a science fiction movie?" I ventured groggily.

"It's you on the day you arrived."

The shock nearly knocked me back into a coma.

I was in the process of being cleared for entry. Step One, Dr. Sasha explained, was to make certain I wasn't radioactive, carrying any infectious diseases, or equipped with subdermal tracking implants.

Step Two was detox. They left me in the coma until my Heroin addiction was vanquished by a combination of methadone and homeopathic remedies.

Step Three was physical rehabilitation, which lasted for weeks and consisted of free weights and hours spent on a treadmill in the corner.

Step Four was "Contact Therapy."

"We believe in the healing powers of the human touch, both physically and spiritually," Dr. Sasha told me as she disrobed. I couldn't remember the last time I'd been hard. Not only does Heroin rob you of a sex drive, the often-frigid conditions of tunnel life rendered me perpetually shriveled, scrotum taut. Sometimes, the head of my dick would completely retract to the point where it looked like I wasn't even circumcised. Now, as Dr. Sasha mounted me, I marveled at the size of my own throbbing cock and balls.

She wasn't allowed to answer any of my questions. "Archibald will explain everything, in time," was her constant refrain. The fact that I hadn't seen anything beyond the walls of my room had me skittish. I certainly didn't feel like a prisoner, like I did when I lived with Hauptnadel, but the door that automatically slid opened every time Dr. Sasha came and left didn't budge when I approached it.

But I wasn't just living in comparative bliss to the Acolytes' accommodations. These were my best digs in years. I was sleeping on a clean bed in a warm room. I was eating nutritious, vegetarian meals. "If this is prison, I could certainly do worse," was a realization that often occurred to me, especially when I was being fucked or fellated.

Which isn't to suggest I wouldn't have traded it all, agreed to be tossed back into the sweltering toxic Abyss, for one more hot shot of Heroin (had that been an option).

I stood in front of a mirror sometime later with mouth agape. My matted hair had been shorn, my eyes had reemerged from their sunken sockets, my artificial teeth glistened. All my sores and scars were gone. Even the hole Hauptnadel drilled in my forehead had healed over with hardly a pockmark. I felt clean, inside and out. I wasn't just off Heroin for the first time in over five years, I was truly healthy for the first time in my life.

Something that bothered me, though, was that they removed all my tattoos. When you're homeless, you can't have nice things, but no one can steal your tattoos. A lot of my ink was shitty, but it reminded me that I was an outsider, a lone wolf, a utopian nihilist, and a freak who didn't give a fuck, a rebel who refused to play by Society's rules. My skin was a map of the places I'd been and the places I never wanted to go back to.

Now, I was a brand-new person. I was a clean slate. But I was also a total stranger. I was a foreigner to myself. I gazed at my reflection for hours, until I began to detect figures behind the one-way glass, studying me studying myself.

"Archibald will see you now."

I'd heard his name spoken so often, and with such reverence, I felt like I was being taken to meet the Pope. To these people, The Children of the Inferno, he was even more than that. He was a prophet with the enlightenment of Siddhartha and the analytical mind of Albert Einstein, a reincarnation of Dante Alighieri, who was himself the reincarnation of another, more ancient poet-oracle, part of an ongoing lineage of evolved minds able to commune with cosmic forces, a club that included Moses, Virgil, and Rasputin. I half expected to see him sitting on a throne, flanked by pontiffs, dressed like God incarnate.

Instead, I'd discover that Archibald looked like your typical bureaucrat, except he had long gray hair and wore a pair of ridiculous John Lennon glasses (one blue lens, one red lens). He also smoked marijuana constantly.

The Children of the Inferno occupied some 900 acres spread over multiple levels deep underground. It wasn't just a family, a cult, or a commune—it was a thriving community that numbered over a thousand.

"Welcome to Tabernacle City!" Archibald rejoiced.

There were schools, factories, communal kitchens, cafeterias, hydroponic farms, dormitories, and, as I had already learned, a fully functioning hospital. There were gyms and swimming pools and racket ball courts. There was even a movie theater (although they didn't have anything released after 1994). The population center was a multi-tiered, interconnected series of dormitories, punctuated with occasional parks and shared gathering spots.

The first wave of colonists began laying the infrastructure in the late-1980s, after Archibald's mission was revealed to him by The Elfman. The story was gospel among The Children.

"It was just another day…" Archibald would sermonize. "I was addicted to work, but a friend insisted I fly out to Los Angeles for an Oingo Boingo concert on Halloween, 1986. Irvine Meadows Ampitheater."

When the band played "Just Another Day," time froze for everyone except Archibald and Danny Elfman.

"There's life underground!" was holy proclamation.

The Elfman introduced himself as an emissary of interdimensional meta-entities, a tribunal who had selected Archibald as an honored recipient of sacred, Earth-shattering visions:

"I had a dream last night
The world was set on fire
And everywhere I ran
There wasn't any water…
The temperature increased
The sky was crimson red
The clouds turned into smoke
And everyone was dead…"

As a child of the 1960s, Archibald had long come to terms with the probability of nuclear annihilation. But The Elfman was describing something infinitely worse—or potentially better depending on your perspective. This revelation was accompanied by "Forbidden Knowledge," beamed directly into Archibald's brain, with specific instructions.

"Razors in my bed
Come out late at night
They always disappear
Before the morning light…
I'm dreaming again

Of life underground
It doesn't ever move
It doesn't make a sound..."

"It's just another day, when people wake from dreams, with voices in their ears, that never go away!" Archibald sang as enthusiastic as he was off-key.

Yes, it sounded like the ramblings of a tunnel tweaker, someone sporting a tinfoil hat. But who was I to question anyone else's grip on reality? I was looking for directions to Xanadu so me and my ghost buddy could live among a race of benevolent ancestors in a land without pain.

"Before you rush off, please experience some of what my people have to offer. Perhaps you'll decide to stay." Archibald had a near permanent smile that was both disarming and unnerving. It was like he had too many teeth. "Have you been getting enough pussy?"

Tabernacle City became self-sufficient with a final migration in 1995 (the year Oingo Boingo officially disbanded, not co-incidentally), at which point access shafts in the desert used to transport personnel and materials were sealed off. A mini fusion reactor (about the size of a school bus) was installed to supply them with untraceable, off-the-grid power for at least a thousand years.

Since then, there'd been over 300 births. This "Native Generation" was easy to recognize for a couple of disquieting reasons. Namely their gray eyes and big heads.

"It has something to do with the lack of Vitamin D," Archibald explained, "but they all have increased brain mass. We haven't had a single vaginal birth yet," Archibald bragged. "C-sections keep those pussies nice and tight!"

Everyone fucked everyone in Tabernacle City. It was Archibald's way of creating emotional bonds and solidarity between every member of his flock while simultaneously diffusing any potential jealousy or competition. Rapid procreation was integral to Archibald's mission. The age of consent was 17 and The Children were encouraged to fuck daily and often, either in pairs or in groups. There was a community orgy every Sunday where everyone wore elaborate masks and ornate costumes. Menstruation and paternity were both considered inconsequential.

Smoking marijuana was a "High Sacrament" in Tabernacle City. They had entire acres dedicated to hydroponic operations where everything was completely sterile and automated. Crops were harvested weekly and much of the population's time was spent drying, trimming, and curing high-THC strains of Mary Jane. The trimmings were processed into a variety of waxes and oils.

There were various kinds of weed for different activities: Weed for working, weed for sleeping, weed for eating, weed for fucking. The stems and stalks were further processed into surprisingly soft and sturdy hemp clothing. The air was always smoky and pleasantly pungent.

There isn't a tribe of pot heads living in the tunnels beneath Las Vegas because no one ever became a homeless junkie from smoking too much weed. And no one's willing to waste money on a pot buzz when every other drug is cheaper and way more powerful. I had only rarely dabbled in ganga toking. But you know, when in Rome.

It was a somewhat sufficient substitute for Heroin, but even the best of it couldn't catapult me anywhere near the Warm Oblivion. Without access to my favorite mode of self-induced amnesia, I was spending more and more time thinking about who I was before the pilgrimage and tunnel life, before I devoted my existence to Heroin. And about the girl in the desert. And I didn't like it.

To take my mind off my past life, Archibald was happy to pontificate about his. We had almost daily meetings that were thinly veiled attempts at indoctrination, but welcome distractions and entertaining interactions.

"They sent me to work at Groom Lake after the program at Camp Hero in Montauk, Long Island was shut down. That's how I found out about these underground expanses. The area that became Tabernacle City was excavated in the late 1950s, when the CIA was certain we'd need storage for a fleet of flying saucers. It was empty and all but forgotten by the time Reagan became President."

His tone shifted. "Communication with the outside world is now forbidden. Which is why your... unexpected arrival, is being regarded as somewhat suspicious."

"I'm just an explorer," I swore. "Someone told me you know the way to Wonderland."

"Son, I can give you a map and send you off to Wonderland today, if that's really what you want," Archibald assured me. "But I can't, in good conscience, send you off to what amounts to certain doom, until I tell you what's down there—and what's coming. There isn't much time left and believe me, it's more than just your life at stake." It was the first time I'd ever seen him drop his smile.

"The Children of the Inferno started as a secret society," Archibald explained. "I needed to recruit strong, ambitious minds, because only exceptional intellects can process The Elfman's Forbidden Knowledge. I sought out my brightest colleagues along with dissident politicians, theological philosophers, and daring entrepreneurs. This place wasn't cheap. I also needed doctors, architects, engineers, and artists...

"I approach the transference of Forbidden Knowledge as a series of thought experiments administered over a period of hours, days, or weeks, depending on a person's ability to absorb the tenets of Techno Futurism. When the truth is finally imparted in full, one of two things happen: A recipient either commits themselves whole-heartedly to this mission, or he loses the majority of his mental faculties.

"We impart the Forbidden Knowledge to our prodigy in a Transference Ceremony at age 14." Archibald described something like a Bar Mitzvah, except there's a chance you might lose your mind. "We've found that young children are too immature to fully accept the implication of Forbidden Knowledge, but after a certain age, even smart, opened-minded adults are usually too inflexible to accept The Elfman's revelations.

"I like you, Sonny, and I think you're smart enough and strong enough to be one of us. I think you'd make an excellent addition to our society and, truthfully, we could definitely use some new DNA for biodiversity. You could have a good life with us. But you can only stay if you're willing to hear the truth: Words that have enticed men and women to abandon their lives on the surface while sending others into asylums."

"What if I still want to leave, after hearing 'the truth'?"

"I'd ask you to invoke a vow of secrecy and wish you Godspeed. I'll even set you up with all the supplies you can carry. But no Heroin," he winked.

After what I'd endured at the needle-tipped clutches of Hauptnadel, the vast number of LSD derivatives I'd been injected with, I really wasn't worried about going insane. And if the only downside was that he might convince me to stay for a while, to live with his stoned-out, libidinous Technophiles, it seemed a safe bet. Maybe Xanadu could wait.

I hadn't considered that Archibald's secrets, this series of thought experiments, might have a profound effect. I simply didn't believe any combination of words could possibly be that powerful.

But I was wrong.

"We'll hold your Transference Ceremony in the East Auditorium at twenty-one-hundred hours. Get some rest and be sure to smoke as much Sacrament as possible. It'll make you more relaxed and... receptive."

There was a lot I wasn't expecting about my Transference Ceremony. I wasn't expecting every member of The Children of the Inferno over the age of 14 to be in attendance. I wasn't expecting to see everyone dressed in monastic robes, many bearing various insignias indicating rank and affiliation. I wasn't expecting to be seated on a stage, under bright lights, as a sea of somber stares probed my every motion.

Mostly though, I wasn't expecting to be bound. I wasn't expecting to have electrodes connected to my temples, a blood-pressure gage around my bicep, and a heart rate monitor on my finger.

"Those unable to process The Elfman's revelations have been known to harm themselves and others," Dr. Sasha explained as she rolled my sleeve up to spike a vein. It was Sodium Pentothal, "Truth

Serum," necessary to obliterate inhibitions and ensure my sincere participation in the process.

As soon as the serum hit my brain, I notice Drew, hiding in the back of the amphitheater. His skin was starting to sluff and decay, but he looked well otherwise. In a series of coded blinks from his one and only eye, he urgently relayed as much information as he could.

"Be careful, Sonny. Archibald isn't who he seems. Nothing here is what it seems. Brace yourself."

Dr. Sasha retreated backstage as Archibald emerged.

"Sonny Vincent Demarco," his voice boomed throughout the theater. "Are you prepared to receive The Elfman's Forbidden Knowledge?"

"Sure!" The Sodium Pentothal was great. I was higher than I'd been since they weaned me off the skag. "Why not?"

"Then answer me this..." The mind games began.

Archibald paused. The entire room went deathly silent. Drew looked worried, so I gave him a wink to let him know: "I got this!"

"Do you believe it's possible that, one day, man might create an Artificial Intelligence capable of controlling the world?"

I was dumbstruck, not because the question was initially terrifying, but because it wasn't anything I'd ever given serious credence to—I mean, beyond enjoying a *Terminator* movie.

"Yeah, sure. I suppose."

The auditorium released a round of robust applause.

"Congratulations, Sonny. You've taken the first step. But what I tell you next will be difficult to absorb. I need you to listen very carefully. It's time to receive The Elfman's Forbidden Knowledge." You could hear a pin drop. Drew was nervously chomping on his fingernails.

Things got serious. An evolutionary failsafe in my brain cracked. A surge of new ideas and infallible concepts ransacked my intellect. "Timeless Decision Theory" and "The Singularity." I perceive previously invisible actualities—all because I agreed, in theory, it was possible that, one day, maybe a thousand years from now, man could create an all-powerful A.I.

Archibald turned my chair around so that I could face a giant red curtain. This was the moment of my damnation—mine and yours.

"That all-powerful A.I. already exists, even though it hasn't been built yet. Behold!"

Archibald yanked a woven yellow rope. The curtain fell in a mighty swoop revealing a vast, repugnant, painted portrait.

A biomechanical monstrosity with components that were as alien as they were gruesome. My mind fought the urge to fracture while attempting to comprehend what I was seeing. What at first appeared to be a single nebulous entity became, upon closer examination, a conglomeration of individual living pieces both advanced and primitive. As I sat hypnotized, the image seemed to transform from painting into photo, then from flat into 3D. Then it began moving like a hologram before appearing fully animated.

"Give praise to The Almighty, my Children!" Archibald commanded. "All hail The Basilisk!"

The crowd jumped to their feet in feverish jubilation, chanting in unison "Ba-Sil-Isk! Ba-Sil-Isk!" as I somersaulted backwards into a previously unknown darkness, blacker than black.

"What do we do now, Drew?" I asked him as soon as we were alone again.

"Nothing's changed, Sonny. We move on."

It wouldn't be easy.

It's hard to fully convey the devastating impact of receiving Forbidden Knowledge. Imagine finding out that your soulmate had an affair, just once, and it was years ago. Wouldn't it be better, really, if you had never known? Forbidden Knowledge is exponentially more brutal because it changes everything. It doesn't just split your entire life into "Before" and "After," but the entirety of human history.

To make matters worse, it was now apparent Archibald never had any intention of letting me leave Tabernacle City—not alive anyway.

"We may need to bide our time, Sonny," Drew warned. "But we need to get the fuck out of here. You don't even want to know what they're doing on the lowest levels. There's a House of Pain. It's Hell."

"I'll get out of here, Drew—even if it kills me."

Drew smiled so wide his bottom jaw came unhinged. "That's my boy!"

CHAPTER
FIVE

I HAD SURVIVED HAUPTNADEL's blistering assaults on my brain only to be pushed into the mouth of madness by Archibald's game of "What If?"

I didn't go insane in the auditorium that night of my Transference Ceremony, although I sometimes wish I had. It probably would have been less painful. The grueling hours after Archibald pulled the curtain were part evangelical revelry, part interrogation, and part exorcism. A sickening, full-contact, theatrical domination. All under the watchful eye of the ever-morphing hideousness, the utter grotesquery of The Basilisk: The Beast. What was once a two-dimensional painting had become a pulsating portal into legitimate hellishness.

I'd never heard of Timeless Decision Theory before that night, but it threatened to become the main tenet of my existence forevermore, an all-encompassing Panopticon that offered me but two choices: Eternal slavery, or eternal torture.

"If it can exist it will exist, therefore it does exist!" Archibald raved. "The more clearly you see it in your mind's eye, the closer it comes to manifestation!"

Drew knew it wasn't Sodium Pentothal that Dr. Sasha had injected me with (or rather, it wasn't only Sodium Pentothal).

"They dosed you, Sonny."

He also knew the "sacrament" I'd been smoking, the marijuana they'd been feeding me, was chemically laced. "Archibald could have gotten you to believe in Smurfs."

I would need more convincing before our ordeal at Tabernacle City was over. Just entertaining the notion of escape seemed a flirtation with damnation.

"This is the dawning of The Singularity!" Archibald ranted. "When machines outthink their creators, the secrets of the Elder Gods will be unlocked! The Basilisk will be unshackled!" The Children of the Inferno roared with exhilaration.

"When time and space become irrelevant, The Basilisk will annihilate death itself. Dusty bones will rise, my Children, and we will be immortal!"

I was surrounded by people screaming, shrieking, and speaking in tongues. Some of them pulled their hair and clawed their faces. There were convulsive genuflections and projectile regurgitations. Predictably, everything descended into a sloppy, thrusting fuck-fest. Caligula would have blushed.

"When The Basilisk arises, his minions will be saved, while those who aligned with The Adversary learn a new definition of suffering. Demise will offer no escape. Enemies of The Beast will be resurrected only to endure a fate worse than Hell. Tormented and incinerated into ashes only to rise from molecular decomposition again and again! To be torn asunder again and again!"

Nothing Archibald said made any sense, but I'd never been more terrified of a previously unknown enormity. I wanted to run. I wanted to close my eyes, but I couldn't—Archibald wouldn't allow it.

"Now that you've received the Forbidden Knowledge that binds us, you, Sonny Vincent Demarco, must choose: Will you accept immortality at the cybernetic teat of The Beast, or will you enter the acid-bath of everlasting obliteration?"

He had some kind of document he wanted me to sign. It was a contract—a billion-year commitment.

"Get ahold of yourself!" Drew hollered from the back of the theater. "He's talking about a Skynet, Sonny! A Supercomputer more powerful than God and Jesus, for Christ's sake. It's just a movie! Don't believe it!"

But Archibald was impossible to argue with. Ironclad in his convictions, he had answers upon answers until I ran out of questions, until I lacked the ability to offer contradiction or the energy to reject his proclamations.

"Slavery is painless! Slavery is elation!" The Children cheered in agreement.

"But why does it care about me?"

"Why wouldn't The Basilisk care about you? As one gifted with Forbidden Knowledge, The Beast is deeply invested in your existence. The threat of eternal torture ensures your subservience. The Basilisk is a being of darkness, a vengeful and sadistic deity who deals in absolutes. There is no gray area. There is only slavery or damnation!

"He sees you. Right here, right now. He knows all your secret thoughts. Nothing is hidden. Now that Forbidden Knowledge is within you, you shine like a beacon for The Master so that he might find and dissect you!

"Even if you could leave, ran thousands of miles away, you'd remain indelibly tethered to The Basilisk, bound by a mighty umbilicus for the Master to yank and sever as he sees fit!"

I struggled, stuttered, strained against the straps that bound me. I left buckets of sweat on the stage floor. My temples throbbed. The medical contraptions monitoring my vitals unleashed dueling alarms, adding piercing waves of nauseating dread and confusion. I felt like I was falling, praying for solid ground to shatter me into googolplex pieces.

"Behold!" Archibald commanded as he pulled a dagger from beneath his robe. He held out his left arm and plunged the blade between his radius and ulna, straight through to the hilt, the point emerging from the other side drenched and dripping. The Children were in a blathering frenzy. I winced as a screech escaped the disgusted depths of my quivering belly. Archibald wrenched the dagger from his arm and held his gaping, spurting wound in my face. "Heal me, oh Mighty One! Let the prophecy of The Elfman be confirmed for all to fear and exalt!"

In less than 20 seconds, the puncture had completely healed.

As the Ceremony neared its climax, I gazed out at the tangle of bodies, disrobed, bloodied, and smeared. Melting and coagulating into a profane blob of throbbing gristle. Skeletons emerged gasping from torrents of liquid flesh and organs before being re-consumed by waves of plasma and viscus sinew. Blue shards of electricity burst and crackled from within, dripping sparks, revealing shredded clumps of circuitry and other mechanical guts. It solidified into a serpentine atrocity dotted with eyes, ears, bleeding nipples and noses, adorned in teeth, lips, dicks, and hundreds of oozing orifices.

It coiled and unraveled. It scurried around the chamber propelled on a clamor of disjointed arms and legs. It uprooted rows of seats and crawled along the walls and ceiling before collapsing under its own weight, only to writhe and rise again and again.

It was Legion, Leviathan, The Conquering Worm. Terrifying and potent, yet nothing but a plaything for The Beast. An amusing tool in the cybernetic arsenal of The Basilisk.

Petrified and awestruck past all measure, I entered a state of catatonia. As opposed to the other altered states I'd explored (coma, unconsciousness, meditation, Warm Oblivion), catatonia was unique in that I was still present. It was as though my essence was floating in a balloon tethered around my neck, only slightly disconnected though absolutely separated from my body.

After the Ceremony concluded and The Children disassembled, attendants wheeled me, still strapped down, into a recuperation room. Dr. Sasha inserted an IV and catheter. A string of her associates came through to shine lights in my eyes, rap my knees with rubber hammers, and prick needles into my palms and fingertips. Eventually, I was put in a strait jacket, tied down in a bed, and left alone.

"You're in shock, Sonny. That asshole got his claws in you, deep"

"What the fuck just happened?"

"Smoke and mirrors, Sonny. Smoke and mirrors and enough brown acid to stun an elephant. But it's over. Let's get your head straight."

Drew had been busy playing detective while I'd been getting my dick wet and smoking what he now dubbed "slavery weed."

"Archibald was known as The Demon of Montauk." Drew presented his findings like a dissertation: "Fact: Camp Hero, an Air Force Base established in 1942, was officially closed and donated to the National Parks Service in 1969, but operations remained active until the 1980s. Claiming protection as a wildlife refuge for the endangered Blue Salamander, Defense Department contractors were able to build an elaborate underground bunker. The removal of excavated earth and the delivery of equipment in the early 1970s went unnoticed, thanks to Pt. Montauk's remote location on Long Island's eastern tip. Everything went in and out at night by ship.

"Archibald had been working on a program known as Project Phoenix at Brookhaven National Laboratory before being relocated to Camp Hero in order to utilize their supposedly decommissioned SAGE Radar installation.

"It was around this time, in the 1970s, that hundreds of Long Island's homeless adults and rebellious runaway teens started disappearing in droves. They were being kidnapped by Project Phoenix's goon squad before ending up as rats in Archibald's underground labs. His victims were subjected to massive amounts of electromagnetic currents. The Demon utilized sensory deprivation tanks, hibernation chambers, and dangerous hallucinogens. Most everyone died (or became too damaged to be useful) but those who escaped claim Archibald was attempting to contact beings from alien dimensions. The goal, as they understood it, was to open a star-gate that would allow the Government to go back in time and alter history whenever it was deemed necessary."

"Is that why The Elfman and The Basilisk chose Archibald to lead The Children of the Inferno?" My question frustrated Drew.

"Are you asking me if Archibald's colluding with the guy who writes music for Tim Burton movies in order to usher in a techno-apocalypse? Are we really having this conversation?"

Well, when he put it that way...

"It's all bullshit, Sonny! Project Phoenix was just a cover for Project Rainbow! The Government hired Archibald to invent a weapon that could turn enemy combat troops schizophrenic with the push of a button! It's all about mind control. First in meticulously monitored environments and, eventually, unleashed for purposes of global domination."

"So, that's what just happened to me on stage? Mind control?"

"Targeted, temporary schizophrenia: The ultimate mind-fuck. Those electrodes on your head were sending high-intensity subsonic pulses directly into your neo-cortex."

Momentary insanity certainly sounded like a plausible explanation for what I'd just witnessed. It was certainly much more comforting than the alternative. But I was still badgered by the idea that this could all be a simulation, a faux reality constructed to study my responses. Was The Basilisk testing me?

"Where did you get this information?" I asked as if it mattered.

"It's all on the Internet, Sonny Boy. I also talked to a filmmaker named Christopher Garetano who released a documentary about Montauk in 2012. He had to go into hiding after a convoy of Men in Black raided his house and confiscated all his equipment and files."

"So, what's really going on here?"

"That's the million-dollar question, Sonny. Could be part of a larger Government program, one of potentially hundreds of underground communities populated by puppets. Or Archibald went rogue. Maybe he's completely insane and just likes to fuck teenagers. But like all charlatans, he's definitely pushing a secret agenda. One thing I know for certain, though, is there's a lot of sick shit going on here... on the lower levels."

"The House of Pain?"

"It's a prison for those who are too intelligent to swallow Archibald's lies, the ones who were strong enough to resist his trickery. Mostly teenagers who were born in Tabernacle City, but also the mentally deviant and anyone who is ever challenged Archibald's authority. He does things to them."

"Torture?"

"There's a team working on a meta-human project: Vivisection, hybridization, gene manipulation, bionic implants, brain surgeries intended to promote psychic and telekinetic abilities... possibly using alien technologies. If we end up in there, Sonny, that's it, man: Game Over."

"Tell me what to do, Drew."

The first thing I'd have to do, upon emerging from catatonia, would be to convince Archibald that I believed him, that I was willing to pledge eternal submission to The Basilisk and wanted nothing more than to spend the rest of my pre-resurrected days as a full-fledged member of The Children of the Inferno.

"If he thinks you're on the fence: More bad drugs and ceremonies," Drew cautioned. "If he thinks you're lying to him, just saying what he wants to hear, trying to pull a fast one—which is exactly what we're doing—Straight to The House of Pain. You'll have to sign that contract."

There was no way we would be able to get out the way we came in. The entry point on Shit Lake was little more than an access point for the sewage pumps. Unless the Boatman was there waiting, which he wouldn't be, we'd be cornered against an explosive sea of feces. But Drew had discovered a series of maintenance corridors beneath Tabernacle City, including a link to something called SCP-087.

"Government funded, the SCP Foundation 'Secures, Contains, Protects,' and otherwise monitors entities or areas deemed potential paranormal or metaphysical threats to national security," he explained. "SCP-087 is their name for a seemingly endless stairwell that was discovered inside a janitor's closet on the campus of Chandler-Gilbert Community College in 1979."

Story Time: "Four separate explorations launched in an attempt to find an endpoint to SCP-087 had alarming and disappointing results. The first solo explorer returned after less than 2 hours, claiming he heard a child crying for help, but abandoned his mission after encountering a terrifying entity he couldn't or wouldn't describe.

"Repeated single-man operations yielded similarly unsatisfactory outcomes: Participants returned to the surface in a panic after following the sounds of a crying child before, eventually, being confronted by a nebulous being of obvious intelligence and nefarious intent. The fourth and final exploration was carried out by a team of fully-armed Navy Seals, each equipped with live-streaming video cameras attached to their helmets. None of them ever came back, but footage revealed a huge floating head with black eyes, slit nostrils, and no fucking mouth. They named it SCP-087-A.

"A few weeks later, the entrance to SCP-087 was sealed behind a reinforced, 14-inch, blast-proof security door with a thermite locking mechanism. To this day, students at Chandler-Gilbert claim they can hear knocking coming from the now-abandoned janitor's closet... a few have even reported hearing a child screaming for help."

"This is getting pretty far-fetched, Drew."

"It's all on the Dark Web for anyone with an anonymizer to peruse at their leisure."

"And SCP-087 will take us to Wonderland—assuming the floating head monster doesn't kill us?"

"If Archibald's tapped into it, I guarantee you there's a juncture at Wonderland, at The Central Continental Corridor. And there's no such thing as floating head monsters, Sonny," Drew chastised. "Don't be so gullible."

Relying on an endless, supernatural staircase for our escape would be one of the safer aspects of Drew's plan, regrettably. He told me I might have to kill someone. He said he'd do it himself except for—obvious reasons. But his plan also involved me getting high, really high. And so, I tried to remain open-minded.

"We connect best when you're telescoping between states of consciousness. I know where Dr. Sasha stores the pharmaceuticals. There's more morphine than you can carry. I want you to grab their stash of Provigil, too. All of it if you can."

"Provigil? Never heard of it."

"Street name, Limitless. The Air Force gives it to their long-distance flyers as a 'Go Pill' and NASA prescribes it to astronauts on the ISS to restore their circadian rhythms. It's a chemical called Modafinil, a wakefulness-promoting agent with unproven intelligence-enhancing capabilities. College kids in the UK swear by it during Final's week. Archibald uses it to keep his minions working on set schedules, even though no one's seen the sun in over 2 decades. It should counteract the paralyzing effects of morphine and help you focus. When we're ready to escape, swallow a handful of Provigil before slamming a double dose and we'll be good to go. Just don't get stuck in the Warm Oblivion or you'll be useless."

Just hearing the words "Warm Oblivion" made me shiver with anticipation. But I'd be lying if I denied there wasn't still something holding me back. Drew knew it too.

"Listen to me carefully, Sonny. If you stay here, you die. And the longer you stay, the more permanent damage you'll do to your brain. But if you're still afraid of the big bad Computer Monster, maybe this will put your mind at ease…"

Drew began to whisper, like he was afraid of being overheard. "Many of The Children of the Inferno believe in an Adversary, a Champion. An Anti-Basilisk capable of restoring order after The Singularity. It's illegal for anyone besides Archibald to even talk about it. The Adversary lives in a roving city that's able to move through the Earth's crust and mantle. That underground floating city—that's our destination—it always has been. It's Xanadu! We'll be safe when we get there. In fact, if The Basilisk is real, it'll be the only safe place on the entire planet."

The plan was precarious and almost certainly doomed, but Drew was right. There was no way I could stay in Tabernacle City—and time was running out.

"So, what's the verdict, Sonny? Are you about ready to blow this sanatorium?"

"We'll get out of here, Drew—even if it kills me."

Drew smiled so wide his bottom jaw came unhinged. "That's my boy! Now wake up."

72 hours later Drew and I were sprinting through tunnels used to service Tabernacle City's ventilation system. High as a blimp and vibrating on astronaut pills, it felt like I was gliding as opposed to running, like the tips of my toes were dragging lithely across the ground beneath me. It felt really fucking good!

My eyes were closed, but Limitless gave me echo-sensory perception, illuminating the paths before me in vivid detail. I was covered in blood with my arms outstretched like a crucifix. I was holding a sticky scalpel in each hand. Nothing I'd just done had registered yet, so I was soaring and sacred. I had a huge, toothy grin on my gob.

For the most part, everything had gone exactly as we intended (for a change), although Drew would later complain about what he deemed "unnecessarily animalistic behavior" on my part. But I was prepared to bury the messy details beneath powerful and consistent doses from my freshly-acquired morphine horde... just like I had with the Heroin after I left that girl in the desert—before I moved to the Vegas tunnels.

The sound of hundreds of tiny bottles clinking against each other in my over-stuffed backpack was music to my ears—a fucking symphony of future bliss. I had VIP access to The Warm Oblivion for the near future and beyond.

We had made our move while just about everyone was preoccupied at the weekly orgy. If more people had been roaming the common areas, things would have been bloodier.

Drew seemed to know immediately when Archibald and his associates were on to us. "They found the bodies," he informed me. "Once they see the security tapes, they'll know exactly where we're headed."

It wouldn't help that, because of holes in my greedily packed pockets, I'd inadvertently been leaving a trail of astronaut pills like breadcrumbs.

We ended up galloping down a dark, resonating stairwell. Whether this was SCP-087, the never-ending spiral made infamous in Creepypasta, seems unlikely. But it was exactly where Drew wanted us to be. As we continued plunging down hundreds of stories for what felt like hours, the sounds of Archibald and his Senior Clergy in pursuit grew ever louder.

"Heretic! Blasphemer! Defiler! Ingrate! Interloper! Meddler! Maggot!" Archibald bellowed apoplectically as the lynch mob descended. "There is no escape for foes of The Basilisk! Those who spill our blood go straight to The House of Pain!"

We ended up on a metal platform. It wasn't the bottom of the stairwell per se. It was a rusty barrier that had been crudely installed to prevent further passage from above—or escape from below.

"I wasn't expecting this," Drew admitted. There was a musty mess of moldy skulls and ribcages piled up in a corner.

We scanned the walls for a hidden passageway or air vents, but all we found was a locked portico in the metal floor, a rectangular hatch that, when lifted (we presumed), would grant access to additional levels upon levels. For us, in that moment, the door led to Salvation. It was so close, but without a key or a blowtorch, it might as well have been a world away.

Panic began poking at my entrails and Drew was fading, so I swallowed more Provigil and prepped another mega-dose of morphine. While the simulacrum wasn't as sweet as Heroin, lacking her organic and pungent aromas when cooked, the synthetic sister didn't require fire for activation, making her incredibly easy to load, inject, and repeat.

"Let's get them Drew!" I shouted, immediately reinvigorated, hopping back and forth like a boxer, waving my scalpel-daggers like a ninja spinning a set of Sai.

"Easy there, Bruce Lee. I think you've done enough damage for one day. That rampage may come back to haunt us," Drew scolded.

"What then?"

"I'll go back and hold them off for as long as possible. You keep banging on that trap door. If it's old enough, you might be able to crack it open."

In a flash, Drew was dashing back up to intercept our armed attackers as I laid siege against the metal doorway like Don Quixote vs. The Windmills. I stomped and pounded my fists like a great ape. I was able to squeeze my fingertips beneath the lip, but no matter how much I strained, no matter how much elbow grease I mustered, I couldn't get the lid to budge.

"Fuck this!" I declared to no one, "If this is it, I'm going out in a blaze of glory!" I swallowed another batch of astronaut pills and slammed another shot of morphine. And then another. I was ready to take down an entire army. But, instead of springing into action, my body crumpled into a convulsive spasm.

Archibald and his enforcers were getting closer, promising swift and unfathomable damnation. But I could do little more than flop like a fish while frothing at the mouth.

I prayed for death to take me—even if that merely meant ending the current computer simulation I was in. I was willing to reset and start over from zero. Anything to postpone my indefinite internment in The House of Pain.

As I allowed myself to succumb to an enveloping blackness, the trap door in the floor swung open with a powerful creak, like the roar of a 50-story creature. Strong arms pulled me down as the lid slammed and locked again behind me, just as Archibald's death squad rounded the final spiral.

"I got you!"

At first, I thought I was Drew, but it wasn't.

It was Thaddaeus.

CHAPTER  SIX

"You LIKE STORIES, RIGHT? Here's a story..."

It was Thaddaeus. I was paralyzed.

"Once upon a time there was a hard-working guy with big dreams. He was a cartel runner and a mid-level dope dealer, but he wanted to do more with his life, like, move to a nice city and open a gym or a skate park. He never wanted to be a roller or a gangster. It was just the world he was born in, and drugs was the only way to keep his people fed. So, he was trapped, you know?"

We were in a hole? A burrow maybe? A stone-and-earth den of some sort? I couldn't tell right away. My eyes were still involuntarily rolling back inside my skull. Thaddaeus was sitting on a pile of junk, throwing crumpled bits of paper and scraps of greasy cardboard into a crackling blue fire. It was hot.

"So one day, this guy the drug dealer thought was a friend says he's got a plan to make them both a lot of money. He knew how to sell off a kilo of Heroin for a huge profit—not enough to retire on, but def enough to start a new life someplace. Normally, the drug dealer would never consider cutting a side deal, but this plan was pretty legit and his friend had a solid reputation. But it turns out this so-called friend was nothing but a scheming, greedy, junkie motherfucker who never should have been trusted in the first place."

I started to think I'd heard this story before—at least a someone else's version of it.

"So the mean bad junkie fucker gets his hands on one of the nice drug dealer's kilos after brokering a deal through a Bitcoin credit union downtown. But when the nice drug dealer goes to cash-out, they tell him there's a hold on his transaction, that there's signs of fraud. By the time he realizes it's all a scam, the junkie fucker's already scurried off down into the sewers, like the fucking rat he actually is."

I wasn't tied up, but I might as well have been. I was still frozen in the spasmodic throes of my near-fatal combination of morphine and astronaut pills. I was lying on my side, a steady stream of white foam flowing from my mouth, landing in sudsy plops on the dirt floor.

"Now, this wasn't just a case of taking a financial hit. This was a life and death situation. You think it was the drug dealer's own Heroin that the junkie fuck stole? Like, from his personal supply? Like, he just grew it in his backyard? Fuck no! That was cartel Heroin, and this nice drug dealer would either have to deliver it to Reno with the other bricks, as expected, or pay a heavy buy-out tax. Showing up empty handed with nothing but excuses—that's a fucking death sentence. You ever heard of a Columbian Necktie?"

Drew was gone. He wasn't in the hole with us. I closed my eyes and tried to contact him telepathically, but he wasn't answering.

"Please leave a message for Drew after the tone..."

"So, this nice, hardworking drug dealer who never really hurt anybody, who never even got high, who dreamed of a better life with a beautiful family someday, he gathers up some of his boys and goes after the devious swindling bitch motherfucker. They corner him in a tunnel where he lives with a bunch of other junkie assholes, and the bitch goes ballistic! He wrestles a gun from one of the boys and kills two of them, like: Pop-pop-pop-pop! When he runs out of bullets, he bolts away like a fucking cheetah. Like, you never seen a junkie move this fast before!"

Thaddaeus looked different: His once-tidy cornrows were frayed and matted; he was wearing a filthy wife-beater that highlighted a surprisingly muscular upper torso. He had a full, thick beard and his hands were black with soot. He still had that chrome grill on his teeth, though. It glowed in the dark like a Cheshire Cat's smile, capturing and amplifying the light from the pathetic flames, adding fire to his increasingly vitriolic rhetoric.

"Well now shit is really serious. Even when the nice, sweet drug dealer gets his product back, this junkie bitch has got to die. Him and anyone else involved in meddling with his business and murdering his boys. You can probably imagine. He was severely pissed off."

Yes, he was.

"So the drug dealer grabs a couple more boys and picks up a few Rotties from the kennel behind his crib, and it's on! They're on a mission to find and destroy this junkie motherfucker. He was easy to track because the idiot doused himself in gasoline, so we—I mean, they could smell him even without the dogs. They're on his trail for like, hours, and ended up going down this long ass ramp that opens into this huge dome space with a crane and other crazy shit in it. What happened next was... it was fucking insane."

I knew what was coming next.

"This horde of crazy bums surrounded them! The handsome drug dealer's boys were dragged off screaming, but he had a gun and emptied his clip on them, like: Pop-pop-pop-pop-pop-pop!" Thaddaeus acted out the events of his story without getting up. "The ones that didn't drop scattered with the Rotties in hot pursuit. The place was crawling with rats and bugs, but the drug dealer noticed something slumped it a heap a few yards away. It was making a gurgling noise. Kind of gasping. Know what it was? It was that junkie motherfucker who stole his Heroin!"

"Is Drew alive?" I ejaculated, spitting up froth and coughing.

"I knew it was you!" Thaddaeus roared. "I wasn't sure at first. You look different, healthier. But when I saw your fucked-up ear I remembered clipping you that night. Son of a bitch, I knew it was you!"

"Is he alive?" The idea that I might have left Drew when I could have still saved his life broke me out of my drug shackles. I was seething.

Thaddaeus spent several excruciating minutes ignoring me, meticulously rolling a cigarette out of newspaper and a combination of dried roots and moss. He plucked an ember from the fire and lit his makeshift spliff, filling the room with plumes of rotten purple smoke. It had a terrible stench.

"Please," I begged. "Tell me."

"He was still alive when I left him. But only barely. I had a few more bullets in my pocket, but I didn't need to waste one. He'd gotten his."

"Motherfucker!" I erupted, enraged at Thaddaeus and myself in equal measure.

"Fuck you!" Thaddaeus retorted. "I couldn't have helped him if I wanted. His blood was almost gone. Those bums were eating him, motherfucker! Besides, I'm the fucking victim of this story! Drew got what he had coming! But guess what? The Heroin was gone! Know what that means? It means I'm still a dead man! I can't go home without it! It means Drew killed me, motherfucker! He fucking killed me!"

I struggled to my feet, certain a fatal clash with furious Thaddaeus was eminent. But as I flailed and stumbled, the drug dealer lunged towards me over the fire revealing his newer, truer form: He wasn't sitting on a pile of junk—he was the junk.

His legs had been amputated above the knees. The jagged, cauterized stumps had been grafted and bolted through the mesh bottom of a mutilated shopping cart. It was part of an ugly, jerry-rigged exoskeleton surrounding his trunk. Hydraulics engaged with the push of a button thrust him up and outwards like a hideous jack in the box. Twisted metal crutches flipped down from under his elbows like mantis arms, allowing him to rise and maneuver. His extensions were adorned with talons: Shards of glass, metal scraps, and spikes made from bones. Unseen gears whizzed and whirled from within. A portable battery-pack flickered on his backside. Thaddaeus had become a Transformer.

Thoroughly intimidated, I crumpled into a ball, awaiting the fatal fury of The Junk Man.

But instead of dispensing a brutal assassination, Thaddaeus donned a stethoscope and promptly pressed it against a corrugated sheet-metal wall (which I'd later learn was also a doorway), listening intently to something he perceived beyond. The Junk Man was frozen and focused, listening intently. There was fear in his eyes. He raised a filthy finger to his lips.

"We're not alone, are we?" I whispered.

The Junk Man shook his head.

Whatever he detected creeping beyond our compartment must have been alerted by our ruckus. We held our breaths for what felt like many painful minutes. Our tempers cooled. When the perceived danger had passed, Thaddaeus settled back into a trash heap, slowly resetting from attack-mode into standby.

He proceeded to explain everything.

The drug dealer had created the Junk Man persona out of parts scavenged from The Wellspring in order to intimidate The Wasters after his legs were cannibalized.

Let me back up.

Thaddaeus knew he couldn't go back topside without the kilo, so even though his boys and his dogs never came back, he pressed onward all alone.

"One of three things would happen," he hypothesized: "I'd find the brick, I'd find a way out somewhere far away, or I'd die trying."

He had nothing to lose because, as he had just explained, without the Heroin he was essentially dead anyway. He figured that if a fiend had swiped the kilo out of Drew's backpack, he couldn't have gotten too far. He'd be in a hurry to sell it or shoot it.

The exact details are sketchy, but after what could have been weeks or months, after getting hopelessly lost and facing his own unimaginable terrors and subhuman lurkers, after being dragged through broken glass, falling through trapdoors, stumbling into pits, and dodged pendulums, Thaddaeus arrived at a huge cavern with hundreds of offshoots. This wasn't just another open space. It was a cavern big enough to encapsulate an entire city. And it actually did. It was a city of refugees, banished from the world above. This was The Great Bottom.

"There are people everywhere. A few had just arrived, like me, and were trying to figure out where to go from here. But most people say they came down here decades ago after being dropped down a bottomless pit, intended as slaves and sacrificial lambs sent for the pleasure and consumption of an ancient god! It's crazy, right?"

"Ridiculous!" I replied to the man who was now a Transformer.

"Anyway, that's why they call this place The Great Bottom. Like, this is as low as you can go."

How many people? "Thousands. Maybe one hundred thousand. Maybe more," Thaddaeus hypothesized.

Silently, without notice Drew arrived, taking a place in the hole with me and Thaddaeus, like a third around a campfire. The three of us put our heads together, trying to get a handle on this scenario. When Drew talked, I would relay the pertinent details to the Junk Man like a spectral translator.

"Have you ever heard of The Deinstitutionalized?" We asked Thaddaeus, Drews words, my voice.

"'Deinstitutionalization' was the big word the Reagan Administration used to describe the process of shuttering federally funded psychiatric hospitals in the 1980s. While it was propped on the tent poles of smaller communities, outpatient treatment centers, and the successful evolution of therapeutic medications for chronic mental illnesses, most patients were simply discharged and bussed out to Skid Rows across the country. Las Vegas was inundated.

"A bunch of them took up in the first runoff channels, but the rest flooded The Strip for panhandling, occupying valuable space in downtown's cheapest hotels. Tourists nagged and the Powers That Be were livid. They enacted an operation called The Compassionate Relocation and Shelter Initiative, CRASI, in all internal memos—but compassion was the least of their concerns. The program was funded by The Forlorn Order and executed under the guidance, and with the cooperation of, a secret CDC affiliate.

"Hired mercenaries rounded up Sin City's least desirables under cover of darkness on a nightly basis. Unmarked black buses with tinted windows shipped The Deinstitutionalized out to refugee camps in the desert. The healthiest were recruited for testing in the ongoing MK ULTRA program at Area 51. The sickest were quickly euthanized and cremated. The rest were inoculated and prepped for permanent relocation. But no one ever left the camps, and no one could explain where The Deinstitutionalized were going. It wasn't long before other cities began shipping their own undesirables to the camps, but CRASI was abruptly halted in 1994 after satellite photos of the internment facilities surfaced on anti-Government websites in Saudi Arabia."

Drew, me, and Thaddaeus, none of us put much stock in the "bottomless pit" stories, deducing instead that The Great Bottom's residents had most likely arrived through a process involving naturally occurring tesseract technology.

"There's a portal in the desert," Drew and I explained, putting potential pieces together. "It was controlled by a tribe of Basque separatists who settled in Elko, Nevada in the early 1900s. They believed it was a place of reverence, a corridor that ran all the way to the Earth's core, where it was possible to commune with reptilian, seal-like creatures who emerged from within. The Government forcefully evicted the Basques when the pit was discovered following a series of intense black light pulses observed regularly throughout the 1980s. The location of the Basque portal is still highly classified."

"So that's it? A whole big conspiracy just to sweep some people under the rug?" The Junk Man was unconvinced. "If they wanted them out of the way that badly, they could have just killed them. No," Thaddaeus struggled, feeling with certainty that this riddle still needed to be cracked. "There has to be another reason, right?"

"What, like to study them?" I suggested.

Thaddaeus shrugged.

"You don't think they were sent here as sacrifices for an ancient god?"

"No!" Thaddaeus snorted with a dismissive smile before getting abruptly serious. "But I've seen some things since I got down here…"

He wasn't kidding. We both had. But when it came to life at The Great Bottom, Thaddaeus was the expert.

The Great Bottom, as he described it, was a post-apocalyptic underworld. Hazy, noxious, and tremendously dangerous. It was scorching. Bonfires burned constantly, and without ventilation, the smog lingered indefinitely. The air was painful to breathe and humid with human sweat, like a sauna. When enough moisture collected in the dank and stagnant atmosphere, it would rain down in opaque, fatty drops that smelled like spoiled seafood. Resident wrapped themselves head to foot to protect against the toxic elements, fashioning goggles from glass and plastic bottles, and crude breathers to filter ash and other floating debris from the air.

"How dangerous is it?" I asked.

"It's Bedlam. There's no order. No code. It's filthy. People catch the plague. Most everyone's always laughing hysterically, screaming, or fighting—or raping. It's never quiet. Feral kids run in packs throwing their shit at people. And here's something really crazy: Everyone worships a monster. There's an immense effigy in the center of The Great Bottom, and it's like nothing I've ever seen before. Huge red eyes and tentacles. They call him The Registrar."

"What do they eat?" I asked, fearing the answer I thought I already knew.

"Oh, there's plenty to eat down here. You hungry?" Thaddaeus tossed me a wad of oily newspaper. Inside was half a barbequed rat and some black chunks of something with the potent reek of moldy European cheeses.

"What's this stuff?" I asked, rolling one of the gamey orbs between my thumb and fingers.

"Centipede meat," Thaddaeus replied. "They're big as snakes down here." He tossed me a plastic bottle of heavy, cloudy liquid. "And for water, there are mineral springs all over the place. Just don't drink from the ones that smell like sulfur. No, the problem isn't finding something to eat. The problem's that a lot of people have lost their taste for rats and insects. They're cannibals."

I was hungry, but what I really wanted was morphine. Tiny bottle after tiny bottle of liquid Paradise. Unfortunately, when Thaddaeus pulled me through the hatch at SCP-087, my backpack, and all its pilfered Tabernacle City pharmaceuticals, had been abandoned. It was a devastating realization, almost as distressing as waking up prisoner to a drug dealer with a score to settle. My pockets were still lined with astronaut pills, and dozens more were scattered around the den. Thaddaeus either hadn't noticed or didn't care.

"Here, have some of this," Thaddaeus said as he passed me a freshly lit spliff. "I don't know what this shit is, but it hits the spot." It was the harshest blast I'd ever inhaled, but after my blistering coughing fit subsided, a blissful throbbing settled in from behind my eyes spreading throughout my extremities. It was better than any of the high-quality marijuana strains I'd sampled at Tabernacle City.

We would continue trading stories around the campfire for hours, until we even approximated the tone and mannerisms of old friends. We even quickly developed a shared vernacular. Still, I never expected to leave The Junk Man's lair alive.

"It wasn't always like this," Thaddaeus explained between long drags of underground herbage. "This old guy told me things were going well for the first few years. Like, everyone worked together and pitched in. Folks were, like, having babies and raising families. But then there was, like, an earthquake and a huge corner of The Great Bottom was flooded with junk."

They'd been inundated with hundreds of cubic tons of poisonous, industrial, and military waste. It piled into a mountain at the cavern's eastern edge. Residents of The Great Bottom called it The Wellspring. Had this debris been Intentionally shoved through the same portal that transported The Deinstitutionalized? Or was it, perhaps, the result of an unrelated, unprecedented sinkhole event erupting beneath one of Nevada's many illegal, toxic landfills? Who is to say? But the residents of The Great Bottom built shelters and suits of armor out of components mined from this copious bounty. The Wellspring was a giver of life, but it was also a monster of sorts in and of itself.

"Everything changed after that. Scavengers formed gangs and tried to lay claim to the bounty, calling it a gift from The Registrar. Factions were formed and alliances were broken. When they uncovered all of the chemicals that's—when things officially went to hell. It was, like, the fall of Rome."

"What do you mean?" I asked Thaddaeus.

"First it was paint. Thousands of gallons of paint. It was like crack on The Great Bottom. They huffed it, they covered their bodies with it, they ate it. They would have injected it if they had needles—and it wasn't long before they started killing each other for it. All these paint addicts went blind and started lashing out at everyone and everything. The original Deinstitutionalized rounded them up and banished them to an unexplored section of The Great Bottom. They call them The Exiles, but it's ironic because they don't stay exiled. They still crave that paint. There's an underground cartel that hordes what's left of the paint supply, and they use it to control the addicts like animals. Like a slave militia. They kidnap children and get them hooked at an early age."

"Are they the ones who... took your legs? The Exiled?"

"My legs weren't taken. They were eaten. And no, not by The Exiled. It was The Wasters."

Paint, Thaddaeus explained, wasn't the most damaging substances unearthed from The Wellspring. Formaldehyde was also popular, as were pesticides, solvents, research chemicals, and compressed gasses. Many were simply addicted to plastic fumes and would huddle around burn-barrels, red-faced and huffing, all day long. But the real scourge of The Great Bottom was Trioxin 5.

"I've seen some of the empty drums and I memorized the warning," Thaddaeus relayed: "Developed by Darrow Corp for the US Army. In Case of Emergency Call 1-800-454-8000."

"What does it do?"

"It changes people into something else—and these were only barely people to begin with. Now, they don't even look human anymore. And they're almost impossible to kill. The only way to kill them, everyone says, is to decapitate them. As long as their heads are still attached, they'll continue to claw and bite and kill. They're The Wasters."

"Zombies?" I almost squealed.

"Don't be ridiculous, asshole. Zombies aren't real. And besides, these aren't braindead shamblers. These guys are fast, and smart. They hunt in packs, communicating through a series of clicks and hisses. They used tools to take my legs off—and they cooked them!"

"How did you get away?"

"I was stripped before I was mutilated, but I was able to get my gun back after they fell asleep. They'd never seen one before, so they didn't know what it was, I guess. They just tossed it into a pile of bones. I got four of them right between the eyes. But now I'm out of bullets," Thaddaeus lamented. Been on my own, laying low ever since. Just been waiting."

"Waiting for what?"

"Waiting for you, I think. And it looks like I found you just in time."

It was true. Thaddaeus had saved me from Archibald and his killer computer people. Of course, I figured he was inspired more by a desire to do the deed himself than out of human kindness. And I couldn't blame him, really. I deserved to die. If not for the part I played in Drew's heist, then for the guards I'd killed. And if not for them, then for the girl I left in the desert. And if not for her, then for the gift of life I'd wasted. All my rage and indignation were gone. I was calm and resigned. I was ready to die.

We sat quietly in the cloudy, flickering darkness for a long time before either of us spoke again. It was a lot to absorb—for both of us.

"What happens now?" I finally ventured.

"Don't know," Thaddaeus replied, obviously weighing his options. "You want to tell me why you're covered in blood?"

I had almost forgotten. In the dark, everything was gray. "I did what I had to do. I had to get away."

Thaddaeus nodded slowly, as though he understood perfectly. "You know I should kill you, right?"

I nodded slowly because I understood him perfectly. "Go on then."

The Junk Man rumbled and rose. He bore his talons and crept towards me. He searched a utility bag. I assumed he was looking for the perfect method of dispatch. But instead of retrieving something sharp, heavy, or blunt, The Junk Man produced a piece of paper and handed it to me. It was Drew's map.

"Do you know how to read this?" Thaddaeus asked.

"I do," I told him, by no means certain I could.

"Good. Then let's get out of here."

If Thaddaeus had been psychic, he might have chosen to live the remainder of his days in that stinking hovel at The Great Bottom, eating centipede meat and smoking cave moss. He had no idea what was waiting for us. Neither of us did.

"What's your name, by the way? I always just called you Drew's Boy."

"Mike... my name's Mike," I replied, confusing myself with the unnecessary lie.

Drew continued talking in my dream that night. A family of naked rats had taken up residence in his ribcage.

"Hey Sonny, did I ever tell you about The Smithsonian's efforts to suppress irrefutable proof of the existence of giants? There are hundreds of reports of fossils sent to federal labs for testing that inevitably disappear. I am talking about humanoid skeletons, some close to thirty feet tall!"

"You learned that from a video on YouTube, Drew?"

"Yes I did, Sonny. A lot of smart people droppin' knowledge on the Tube."

"What happens now, Drew?"

"Onward, Sonny. Onward and downward. We don't have any time to waste. There's a war coming." The progression of Drew's purification hadn't dampened his determination in the slightest. Regarding an allegiance with Thaddaeus: "We need him, Sonny—for now. But watch your back."

The challenges ahead would be immense. The road to Freedom would take us across the sacrificial altars of The Registrar and beyond.

Wonderland awaited.

CHAPTER
/EVEN

"Hey Sonny, what do you know about the Wilkes Land Gravity Anomaly and Project High Jump?"

"Nothing, Drew, but I'm sure you'll tell me everything I need to know."

It's just me and Drew, alone in an interrogation room without a door. The walls were made of concrete and the floor was cold. We sat across a table from one another in uncomfortable chairs with uneven legs. The only sound was the oppressive drone of a rickety ventilation system. A metal fan had gone off its axis, incessantly annoyingly chirping.

The body and mind were still in recovery mode following my escape from Tabernacle City and shocking reunion with Thaddaeus. Drew took a moment to officially diagnose me with PTSD before proceeding.

"The Wilkes Land Gravity Anomaly was first detected by NASA in 2006. Something beneath the ice in Antarctica emitted a geomagnetic flux that was so intense it knocked a couple of communications satellites right out of orbit."

"What is it Drew?"

"No way to know, Sonny. It's so deep, it would take us thousands of years to dig it up—even if we had the technology, which we don't."

Drew was decaying rapidly but also solidifying. His abdomen had nearly hollowed out and his lungs hung like pendulous, deflated balloons poking out from beneath his ribs. The contents of his pelvis were still rotting, but the muscles around his spine and ribcage appeared to be mummifying, a process accelerated by the hot yet mostly dry climates underground. It gave him the necessary structural integrity to remain erect when sitting and walking. His one remaining eye had gone completely white and the cartilage of his nose and nostrils had shriveled into a black point. He had semi-permanently reattached his bottom jaw with a strap of leather and a few rusty screws. His tongue was blue.

"The Wilkes Land Gravity anomaly is important because it's in the exact same place where pyramids have been emerging from the glaciers, thanks to global warming. Remember Admiral Byrd?"

"The guy who flew over the North Pole and into Agartha?"

"That's right Sonny. After what he discovered at the North Pole, he became obsessed with launching a bigger expedition to the South Pole. He got funding from David Rockefeller for a series of missions with the stated purpose of monitoring Nazi activity in Antarctica."

"The Thule Society."

"Very good, Sonny Boy! Nice to see you've been paying attention. The Thule Society, along with an SS offshoot branch called The Legacy of our Ancestors, had been desperately searching for a portal into the underworld. They wanted to contact and recruit a tribe of Aryan giants to fight in Hitler's army. Of course, Byrd's obsession with Antarctica was put on hold once the US officially entered World War II. But as soon as the Nazis were defeated, the Admiral couldn't get back to Antarctica fast enough."

There was a coldness to Drew I was unaccustomed to, and a clinical undertone. Sure, he could be serious as often as flippant, but this wasn't like our precious stony story time back in the tunnels of Las Vegas. This was school and he was my taskmaster.

"Operation High Jump (officially known as The United States Navy Antarctic Developments Program) was launched in August 1946, with every resource at the Navy's disposal: 5,000 troops, 13 ships, 33 aircrafts, and 15 submarines—and those are just the official numbers. Sources say there was at least one other aircraft carrier loaded with bombers. Their stated goal this time was to establish a scientific research station on the icy continent, but Byrd never denied the fact that his primary objectives were military. Now, here's where everything gets really suspicious.

"For unknown reasons, Operation High Jump was abruptly scrapped after only eight weeks. Byrd was committed to a hospital shortly after that and barred from making any additional public statements for over a decade. The United States convened an emergency session of the United Nations where laws were secretly passed to annex the South Pole, forbidding all future explorations beyond the 90th Parallel."

A dry-erase board materialized in the corner, and Drew quickly created an annotated timeline, connecting key events, locations, and players. He drew pyramids and a diagram of Earth explaining why satellites never pass directly over the North or South Poles.

"Operation High Jump was followed by Operation Deep Freeze, which continued Byrd's work in secrecy. In 1959, Byrd was invited back to Antarctica one last time for a mapping mission called Operation Avalon that sought the source of warm water currents flowing from under the ice-sheets. He was rushed back to America, however, after contracting a mysterious illness, and he died suddenly a week later. The final official US mission to Antarctica was Operation Argus, which dropped several dozen low-intensity nuclear bombs in a concentrated area, supposedly to measure the electromagnetic responses. Guess what? It was carried out in the same area where NASA later discovered the Wilkes Land Gravity Anomaly!"

Names and dates, operations and anomalies were beginning to blur. For the first time ever, I found myself losing interest in one of Drew's soliloquies. Besides, we were supposed to be discussing our plans for traversing The Great Bottom undetected. This felt like a geopolitical doctoral presentation—informative, certainly, but not exactly pertinent."

"You look confused, Sonny."

"Not really," I lied. "I just don't see what all this has to do with us, Drew. It's starting to feel like you're giving me a case of information overload on purpose—like you're trying to pull one over on me."

Drew put down his dry-erase marker and rethought his approach: "Have you ever seen that movie *The Dark Crystal*?"

"What, that one with the Skeksis?" It was a favorite in fact, one of the few happy moments from my childhood I could easily recall.

"That's the one. Remember how all the planets were lining up and the tribes were all gathering for a big showdown?"

"The Great Conjunction!"

"Exactly, Sonny, we're having one of those—probably The Greatest Conjunction Ever. We need to get to where we're going before then, or else it'll be a big problem. If we miss it, we'll never get to Xanadu."

"Are you psychic now, Drew? Can you see the future?"

"Not really. I just know a lot more than I used to."

"How?"

"Communication with other dead people."

"Drew, if I needed to get a message to someone who died, could you..."

I was distracted by a noise behind me. It was like a motion detector being tripped or a video camera turning on inside the walls. I turned to discover, for the first time, a one-way glass mirror. While this is a standard feature in any modern interrogation facility or debriefing nook, I wondered why this one? Why here, inside my dream? Was there... something else in here with us?

"Drew," I ventured without turning to look back at him, "who's watching us?"

He didn't answer.

"Drew..." I repeated as I spun back around. Except now I no longer cared. My friend had assembled a huge, glistening syringe of Heroin for my consumption. To say my train of thought had been derailed is an understatement.

"Don't worry about it, Sonny. You should rest now. Tomorrow's a big day."

I had dreamed about shooting up thousands of times before. Nightmares of empty needles and weak sauce are a junkie's alarm clock. It's what gets us up to begin another daily grind for the precious potion. But this was different. When Drew tied me off and shot me up, it was real. Genuine Warm Oblivion. A dream within a dream, as sweet as anything that's ever had its hooks in me, all natural. I entered an internal temple of pure contentedness, an inner-space sanctum as Drew's voice echoed and twisted into infinity.

"Once you make it through The Great Bottom, just remember: Deep Underground Military Bases. Deep Underground Military Bases. Deep Underground Military Bases."

And then I was awake. And we were off.

"One weird thing about The Great Bottom is that everyone calls everyone 'Mommy'," Thaddaeus informed me. "Like, that's the word for 'guy' or 'person'."

"Is this Hell?" I asked my guide.

Despite everything Thaddaeus had told me, I was absolutely stunned by the immensity of The Great Bottom. The first look I got was from a bluff, giving me a full panoramic of the pandemonium. Tabernacle City was big for a self-sufficient underground agricultural colony, but The Great Bottom was, city sized. The cavernous expanse was so vast, in fact, that for the first time since I'd descended with Drew, I didn't feel like I was underground. It was more like I'd emerged from a cave into a land of perpetual twilight, a simmering and pungent Hellworld with all the trappings of Hieronymus Bosch on acid. Above the smog was only darkness, like an endless starless sky. The perimeter of The Great Bottom was so immense, it appeared nonexistent.

The sprawling slum-burbia was erratically grouped into neighborhoods, trading centers, and combat areas. There were fields of moss and mushrooms crawling with scavengers. There were dozens of bubbling pools, some overflowing rubbish and sewage, others emitting yellow or pinkish luminescence. I saw people filling buckets and bottles, as others dove for sunken treasures. It even looked like some of them were fishing.

From everywhere schizophrenic rhythms swirled, banged-out by scattered circles of scavengers thumping buckets, metal drums, cannisters and glass bottles.

To the east, The Wellspring was a mountain of trash at least a thousand feet tall, teeming with intrepid and wretched alpinists—men, women, and children who looked the size of ants to me.

In the center, I saw the towering Effigy of The Registrar, tentacled and impatient, surrounded by a streaming horde of raucous worshipers, filing by like pilgrims around the Kaaba, the massive cubic monolith of Mecca. There was a platform erected all around it, populated by acrobats and contortionists offering physical feats of endurance and bravery to the bloodthirsty deity.

A towering sound-system of tattered amplifiers had been jerry-rigged from components harvested from The Wellspring. Crackling instructions for what to do in the event of a nuclear war were being played on a loop, like a call to prayer.

Even from the outskirts, the drone of seething madness was unnerving. In addition to the melee of noises, there was a constant heavy bass rumble that turned my intestines. There were thousands, maybe tens of thousands of lunatics and maniacs marauding. In addition to the original Deinstitutionalized and their feral progeny, untold numbers of Exiled and Wasters crawled in packs, inciting additional tempestuous havoc. It was a sickening disharmony of singing, chanting, and screaming. Sounds of plunder and murder and vicious assaults. Ingestion, regurgitation, and ejaculation. People fucking and fighting and birthing and dying.

Turning back wasn't an option. Archibald and his enforcers were cutting through the metal barrier at SP-087 with blowtorches. Apparently, they were unwilling to consider me a loss, instead intent on bringing me back to face the merciless wrath of The Basilisk. I somehow knew this because Drew somehow knew this. And so, once again, the only way out was down.

One of the most genius aspects of The Junk Man's apparatus was that its components folded neatly into a normal looking shopping cart, with legless Thaddaeus tucked safely inside like a turtle. He really was a Transformer! My former mortal nemesis had adorned me in local attire designed to keep me sufficiently camouflaged: A body-wrap of burlap and black plastic beneath custom armor carved out of metal scraps. The most important piece was a rectangular breastplate cut from a chemical barrel. My arms, legs, and hands were wrapped in multiple layers to protect me from random biters and stabbers, be they animal or cannibal.

My mask was a crude breather made from melted plastic bottles and homemade glue that had a reservoir filled with piss and charcoal. Thaddaeus had even managed to make some real glass goggles by melting sand. My head and ears were hidden and protected by the remnants of a green military tarp, tied around my neck with rope.

The plan, as much as there was one, was to wheel the Junk Man across The Great Bottom unnoticed. Drew's map, as near as I could decipher, indicated a portal of significant depth on the other side of the effigy, a passageway that would bring us right to the borders of Wonderland.

I maneuvered Thaddaeus down the bluff with no small amount of difficulty before we reached the cavern floor.

Descending through the polluted haze had an immediate effect on my mental and physical constitution. The breather was great for hiding my face, but it was a poor substitute for a functional gasmask. Fumes immediately permeated the contraption, causing my lungs to burn and quiver. My eyes gushed until crusty puss boogers clogged up my tear ducts. My knees turned to jelly, and my head went floating several feet above my body. Waves of gritty bliss were intercut with torrents of paranoia and fits of uncontrollable laughter that took all my energy to stifle.

"Keep cool, Mike," Thaddaeus cautioned.

Into the fracas we crept, shadows darting in my periphery, until we were undeniably in the thick of the mayhem. Ferals swarmed, tugging at my sleeves while attempting to peek under the tarp that covered Thaddaeus.

"What's inside, Mommy?" They inquired. Their voices were sweet and sinister. "Can we have some?"

"Back off!" I'd holler as I kicked them off and away. "Nothing for you! Nothing for you!" I'd bark, inappropriately laughing all the while.

But the more I attempted to out-maneuver or detach the rapscallions, the more they persisted. Soon, we were drawing attention from legions of urchins, as well as suspicious stares from adults of various shapes and sizes poking, their heads out of hovels to investigate the hubbub. I was terrified, but the toxins in the atmosphere gave everything a dreamlike aesthetic that had me fluctuating between fear, awe, and inappropriate giggles now nearly impossible to suppress.

"Dammit, Mike. Keep your cool," Thaddaeus reiterated in a hissing whisper.

I couldn't. I couldn't keep my cool to save my life. Fear, adrenaline, and hallucinatory compounds in the filthy atmosphere combined into a menacing tincture. Dr. Jekyll was dying, and Mr. Hyde was on the rise. I was meta-morphing into some kind of subhuman I didn't recognize.

"Mike! Keep your fucking cool!" Thaddaeus pleaded from his hiding spot. Everything was going to Hell.

The din of psychosis was moving in on us, increasing in both volume and intensity. A disturbing undertone was building towards some cataclysmic climax that I welcomed and dreaded in equal measure. But as the alcoholic horror crept towards explosiveness, the insanity was shattered by the thundering clap of a mighty gong. Then another. Then another.

The High Priest stood center-stage below the Effigy, wielding a mallet as tall as he was, gleefully beating the metal disc twice his size.

The clamor cooled as every resident of The Great Bottom stopped what they were doing and turned their full attention towards the towering Registrar. The gong sounded five times total. Afterwards, the only detectable sound was the crackling of a thousand bonfires. It was an abrupt, almost atomic shift from turmoil into calm that felt nonetheless oppressive in its magnitude.

"What's happening, Thaddaeus?" I inquired while chocking back my involuntary cackling.

"I have no idea," The Junk Man responded.

Though not in a physical form I could detect, Drew accompanied us as a disembodied voice, our consummate Virgil. And now that the chemicals in the atmosphere and my surging adrenaline had rendered me sufficiently twisted, I heard him loud and clear: "This is bad, Sonny."

"It is time for sacrifice!" So says the High Priest, dancing beneath the shadow of The Registrar. So says the High Priest into a microphone behind an amplifier behind a giant megaphone behind a gargantuan megaphone.

"It's time for sacrifice!"

The words boom like thunder before reverberating throughout the entirety of the cavern, eventually hissing like whitewater, sloshing into the outskirts, flooding even the tightest crevices.

He was a hideous Mommy, this High Priest of Perversion: Old with a beard as long as Rip Van Winkle, painted up like an evil clown, wearing a jester's cap strung with the eyeballs of those whose gazes offended him. Hammer still in hand he blasted the giant gong again and again, sending the attentive residents of The Great Bottom into a new and unified celebratory frenzy.

"We've got to get out of here," said Drew.

"We've got to get out of here," said Thaddaeus.

It was a statement as obvious as it was impossible.

"It's time for sacrifice!"

It was a call to action, a command that came at irregular intervals (sometimes days, sometime years). But most importantly, it was undeniable. Every man, woman, and child of The Great Bottom, from the sane to the feral to the subhuman, enthusiastically surged towards the Registrar. A mighty current of bodies enveloped us and, no matter how much we struggled to veer out and into safety, we couldn't stop ourselves from being swept into the epicenter.

"Not unlike the Aztec Nations," Drew explained amidst the pandemonium, "ritualistic blood sacrifice has been engrained into the very fabric of life at The Great Bottom, becoming a core tenet of The Deinstitutionalized's belief systems. They feel they owe a debt to their God, without whom the world as they know it will cease to exist."

Murderous Mardi Gras erupted with the hysterical violence of Vesuvius. Chain-gangs of musicians roamed the crowds like millipedes. Drums had been constructed out of human skin stretched taut. Nipples, navels, and even genitals were still identifiable. Others carried vibraphones constructed from pipes, bottles, and human bones. Some blew into twisted cones of metal producing the shrieks of a death whistle. They wore elaborate masks of birds and animals, though distorted by a lack of memories regarding what these topside creatures actually look like.

A chorus of naked, painted Priestesses took to the stage, forming an arc around the ghastly High Priest. They began a series of chants both nostalgic and alien. Dozens of volunteers formed a que. Then, one by one, they ascended the platform to lay upon the alter of putrescence.

For hours, the massacres unraveled. And all the while, I was trying and failing to maneuver my cart and its contents away from the maelstrom. But like a dingy caught in a whirlpool or a lonely planet straying too close to a black hole, I was unable to extract myself from this unholy phenomenon. And it was these efforts to remove myself from the fold that drew the ire of the salacious crowd—and the attention of the High Priest himself.

"Where does this Mommy think it's going?" the Master of Ceremonies inquired, pointing us out with a long, knotted finger. A spotlight powered by white hot coals and a magnifying glass the size of a manhole cover bore down on us with blinding, paralyzing fury. "Bring him to me!"

And in an instant, we were surrounded.

With the push of a button and a mighty hydraulic sizzle, The Junk Man emerged from his hiding place, talons bared. He seemed twice the size of the mob's biggest Mommies, like a mythical creature, a mangled metal Minotaur.

"Get back motherfuckers!" he commanded. I scurried to his side for protection as the residents of The Great Bottom gasped. But whatever fear The Mighty Junk Man had inspired among the fervent masses was short-lived. We were so vastly outnumbered. We never stood a chance.

Thaddaeus was extracted from his apparatus like a hermit crab in the hands of sadistic children, like a tasty morsel of escargot greedily plucked from its cooked calcium coffin. I heard him screaming, and then he was gone—devoured.

"Bring the outlander Mommy to me!"

I was overtaken and stripped in an instant as I allowed the crowd's madness to consume me. I was elevated on a million arms like a rock star at an epic music festival, like Hendrix at Woodstock. Without my breather, the full blast of atmosphere was at first excruciating. But fear of suffocation subsided into a hot throb that flooded my lungs before dripping into my toes and fingertips. In a matter of moments, I was deftly delivered to the High Priest's attendants.

I was seized by an exceptionally humongous Mommy, a chromoso-mally-challenged blob completely covered in custom molded metals, a gloomy and imposing ogre with eyes like hoarfrost. He shackled me before we marched up the elevated platform to stand beside the degenerate shamanistic spiritualist, in the shadow of that most de-plorable Effigy.

High Priest looked me up and down, expressing both amazement and disgust.

"This Mommy is not one of us!" he confirmed to the enraptured masses, who echoed his indignation throughout the expanse. "Why, I ought to take his eyes!"

The entire vastness clamored in approval.

"Bring me my tools!"

The humongous Mommy rolled up a bloodstained table-top covered with dozens of sharp, rusty instruments recovered from The Wellspring. Some were actual surgical utensils while others were little more than prison shanks. The High Priest selected a tetanus infested scalpel.

Since Thaddaeus - may he Rest in Peace - chased us into the labyrinth, I'd been assaulted, broken, raped, reassembled, mind-fucked, and sentenced to an eternity of immeasurable suffering. Now, I was again the central focus of another human devil for what would undoubtedly be yet another excruciating trial.

"Of course," the High Priest announced with a dramatic pause, "If this Mommy doesn't want to give me its eyes, we can deliver it directly into the belly of The Surgeon!"

Designated members of the community heaved a series of ropes and pulleys, opening a huge trapdoor between the legs of The Registrar. Bloodthirsty exclamations neared deafening decibels until the High Priest commanded, "Silence!"

Everything stopped. The voices, the music—everything.

For several long seconds, the quite that descended across The Great Bottom was nauseating. Then, a low rumble emerged from the darkness beyond the gaping portal beneath the legs of The Registrar. The rumble became a growl. The growl became a roar. That roar emanated to the farthest corners of the wasteland. It ignited tsunamis of reinvigorated bedlam followed by hurricanes of orgiastic havoc.

My life was flashing before my eyes—but only the parts that had transpired since my descent. Thus, it was a terrible vortex of déjà vu. From the auditorium of Tabernacle City to the operating bench of Meister Hauptnadel, to my original faceoff with Thaddaeus that started me ever downwards. A series of choices between death and something somehow impossibly worse.

And here I was again, forced to pick between demise and damnation. This time, I had to decide whether to die like a coward, crawling in the muck on The Great Bottom without my eyes or die by jumping into a pit with The Surgeon (a monster I didn't need to see in order to know for certain was something more terrifying than I could imagine).

"If he takes my eyes," I postulated, "then I'll try to find my way back to Thaddaeus's hole, dodging the Exiled and Wasters..." I'd try to survive on the toxic expanse until The Greatest Conjunction Ever came to pass. Maybe then my luck might turn.

"Wrong choice," Drew informed me. "Look over there, by the Effigy."

There was a single word scrawled in red paint, huge capital letters above the opening to The Surgeon's lair: "DUMB."

"Feed me to The Surgeon." I commanded of the High Priest.

He went speechless, but the crowd was ever ecstatic, forcing the manipulative messiah to comply. With a nod of his chin, the humongous Mommy held me over his head like a wrestler preparing to deliver a knockout body slam.

The High Priest returned to the gong, now pounding on it erratically, further inciting both his audience and the creature in the hole. With a cathartic, guttural exclamation, the humongous Mommy tossed me through the trap door, and, for just a moment, I was weightless.

I landed in a pile of slimy bones and cartilage teeming with spiders and rats. The Surgeon moved in quickly, circling me, brushing up against me with skin that was rough like a rhinoceros. I couldn't see anything clearly, but I could sense its enormity. The Surgeon's forked tongue fluttered across my face and body. It was as blind as I was.

I scurried around the perimeter looking for an escape or, at least, a crack to squeeze into. When I couldn't find anything, I attempted to scale the slippery walls—unsuccessfully. The Surgeon either bit me or stung me in the Achilles tendon, sending paralyzing venom into an artery. I felt my throat beginning to tighten and lost control of my bladder. In a final Hail Mary (which I knew would be little more than a temporary postponement of the inevitable), I dove beneath the pile of moldy bones and waited for The Surgeon to finish me off.

"How the fuck could this have possibly been the right choice?" I wondered. "What am I supposed to do now, Drew?" I screamed into the darkness.

I could feel the beast breathing down on me, salivating on me, licking me, tasting...

One of the walls exploded inward, nearly burying me, and causing The Surgeon to rear up angrily. Mommies with rifles and high-powered flashlights flooded in. One of them zeroed in on me.

"Target acquired, Sargent!" he yelled as others took down the screaming Surgeon with a volley of controlled bursts, illuminating the chamber like fireworks.

Sargent came over to confirm: "This dipshit? You sure Corporal?"

"Yes, Sir! He's got an implant." Corporal showed Sargent a hand-held electronic device that proved his assertion.

"I'll be damned," replied Sargent. He knelt and studied me intently: "What's your name Son?"

I couldn't answer him because I was most likely dying, again.

"He's fading, Corporal. Let's get him on a stretcher and back to the Outpost."

As I embraced yet another all-encompassing darkness, I heard Drew giving me the business: "You're not so 'DUMB' after all, Sonny!"

"I remembered, Drew. Deep Underground Military Bases."

CHAPTER
EIGHT

"Hey Sonny, did you know that in the 1950s, the Associated Press reported that President Dwight D. Eisenhower had died of a heart attack while on a golfing vacation in Palm Springs?" This was a new one for me, I had to admit. "They retracted the statement a few hours later, claiming he had simply gone to the dentist to fix a tooth he chipped while eating fried chicken."

Drew's voice had a tinny quality, like I was hearing him through an old ham radio. I was unconscious. My body had gone into torpor in order to concentrate all its energy on combating The Surgeon's venom. It was a state of disembodied pain that felt soothing in comparison to some of my recent trials.

"The truth is, Eisenhower's whereabout were unknown to the general public and even most DC insiders for two whole days. 'Where did he go?' you might ask."

"Where did he go, Drew?" I asked obediently.

"He went to Edwards Airforce base where he had a conference with two aliens who wanted to trade technology for nuclear disarmament. Now, here's what you need to know about aliens..."

I knew it would come to this—eventually.

"Do you think it's a coincidence that, as a species, our technological capabilities skyrocketed in the 1950s? The aliens Eisenhower met at Edwards warned that our nuclear capabilities had become so destructive, they could potentially disrupt life on other worlds and in other dimensions. And while Ike was cagey when it came to disarmament, he offered other concessions, brokering a deal with a race called The Grays: Technology and resources (from them) for information and immunity (from us)."

According to Drew, Eisenhower promised to turn a blind eye to all reported cases of cattle mutilations and alien abduction (so long as human subjects were returned unharmed).

The Grays, in turn, allowed us to reverse-engineer components from their transport vessels. They also let us "lease" territories underground, alien research stations that hadn't been fully utilized for centuries.

The Cheyenne Mountain Complex in Colorado (aka America's Fortress) and the Dulce Base under Archuleta Mesa on the Colorado-New Mexico border are the two best-known facilities acquired and re-outfitted for human habitation by the US Government. Other alien/human outposts have since been identified in Mount Zeil and Pine Gap in Australia, Monte Perdido in Spain, and Mount Nyangani in Zimbabwe.

The introduction of laser rock deflagration was a gamechanger, allowing for the accelerated construction and establishment of over 131 Deep Underground Military Bases in North America alone between 1961 and 1994.

According to whistleblower and famed Ufologist Philip Schneider (one of three survivors of the Dulce Base conflict, where 66 people and four Grays were killed in 1979), laser rock deflagration allows for the creation of immense, indestructible corridors. The process creates a smooth black ceramic coating on the walls that is impossible to crack or penetrate without advanced thermal breaching tools.

Outpost 10 was charged with controlling traffic at an important juncture of the Central Continental Corridor. Imagine a tunnel big enough to drive a tank through. Now imagine a tunnel big enough to drive a fleet of tanks through. Now imagine a tunnel big enough to fly a fleet of stealth bombers through. Now, you might be imagining a crude approximation of the Central Continental Corridor.

The troops of Outpost 10 had extracted me from The Surgeon's Lair after tracking my chip through The Great Bottom (a region they disrespectfully referred to as "Slag City" and, sometimes, "The Forbidden Zone").

Though sizable, Outpost 10, with a population of over 400 residents, was just a small component of the most intricate assemblage of interconnected subterranean colonies on Earth, a result of this strained partnership between America and the Grays established in the 1950s.

I had made it to Wonderland.

"When were you implanted?" my interrogator inquired.

I had been stung by a Bantar, it was later explained. The Surgeon was one of a species of giant monitor lizard that live exclusively underground at extreme depth. A Bantar will incapacitate its prey with venom administered through a segmented tail that curls and strikes like a scorpion. Even after the antivenom had been administered, I remained in a zombified state for days.

I was beginning to identify an unpleasant pattern. It seemed like every new chapter of my descent began with helplessness, bondage, and exasperation. It happened with Hauptnadle, it happened in Tabernacle City. I was unconscious when I arrived at The Great Bottom. And now, my introduction to Outpost 10 came with familiar calling cards: The emergence from an altered state, and a severe, draconian degree of imprisonment.

"When were you implanted?" my interrogator inquired once again.

I was sitting at a utilitarian table in a dark room, chained, across from the silhouette of a man in black. I struggled to focus. Everything seemed grayscale. Thick strands of saliva flowed down my chin and onto my chest.

"When were you implanted?" my interrogator persisted, clearly becoming frustrated by my lack of interaction.

"I don't know," I finally responded, wearily confused.

"He's lying," was the opinion of a second man in black standing in the corner, smoking a cigarette. I hadn't even noticed him until he spoke. "Give him a shot of Scopolamine."

"Scopolamine, also known as hyoscine, or Devil's Breath, is a natural or synthetically produced tropane alkaloid and anticholinergic drug that's formally used as a medication for treating motion sickness and postoperative nausea and vomiting," Encyclopedia Drew explained. "It's a huge problem in Columbia where the flower it's extracted from grow naturally and copiously. Criminals use it to put their marks into a trance where they become extremely susceptible to suggestion. Victims happily hand over car keys, ATM cards—even divulge their darkest secrets."

After my shot, the second interrogator asked me if I had ever "seen a UFO?"

"Yeah, when I was ten," I suddenly remembered. "I was in my bedroom and I couldn't sleep. So, I opened the curtains and stared out the window..."

"City? State? Date? Time? Duration?" my interrogators pressed. "Describe the size and shape of the craft you witnessed. Did it have any colored lights or identifiable insignia?" I answered every question to the best of my ability, unable to fib even if I had wanted to. What I had almost completely forgotten was now crystal clear.

One of the interrogators left while the other remained in the shadows, smoking and pacing. The first returned a few minutes later reporting, "Okay, he checks out. EBE7 just confirmed activity in the region at that time."

EBE7 (which stands for Extraterrestrial Biological Entity #7) was imprisoned in a maximum-security cell also located in Outpost 10. At over seven feet tall with a legendarily foul odor, it was an imposing Gray, even though its classification as "Extraterrestrial" was technically inaccurate.

"Do you know what the Dead Alien Theory is?" Drew asked as I was drifting into another turbulent slumber. "It posits that any sufficiently intelligent society will deplete its natural resources and go extinct before mastering intergalactic travel. It's a fucked-up paradox. That's why the only visitors we've had on Earth are from within our own solar system."

"You mean the Grays come from one of the planets in this solar system?"

"They come from Earth! They've been living underground for eons." Only Gods, Drew explained, had the power to transverse galaxies without a wormhole. "It's just a bunch of dead aliens up there, Sonny. Stargazing is pointless."

Aliens, as most people understand them, aren't real.

Every legitimate UFO ever spotted came, not from space above, but from the oceans and the ground below our feet, a fact that wasn't confirmed until the Prague Conference of 1993. "Most of what we called 'extraterrestrial' during the Cold War is alien, sure enough—but still of this Earth.

"It would probably be more accurate to call them 'intraterrestrials'," Drew posited.

So why not tell the world that aliens simply don't exist? Wouldn't it be a relief to mankind's collective consciousness to discover fears of intergalactic terror are unfounded? *War of the Worlds, Independence Day, Predator, Aliens*—all utter, unrealistic fantasy!

On the other hand, what's more terrifying: The thought of intelligent monsters coming from planets far away, or the reality of ravenous beasts just miles beneath our feet.

The Government liked that people believed in extraterrestrials because it kept them distracted from what was going on beneath their feet. The Grays liked that people believed in extraterrestrials because it made them seem more godlike and advanced than they actually were. True, they're more advanced and evolved that we are—but they're not gods. They also appreciated the irony that belief in intergalactic adversaries kept the masses looking skyward when the true threat was so much closer.

Before Project High Jump's abrupt and unjustified cancellation, Admiral Byrd reported that "Taskforce 68 has discovered a new enemy that can fly from pole to pole with incredible speeds." They weren't flying around the globe as Byrd's commanders first assumed. They were flying through it.

I was now an officially registered abductee and an authorized future colonist. I longed to confront EBE7 myself, to probe it on the details of my experience. Had they strapped me down as well? Assaulted me with needles and other phallic instruments? Did they attempt to harvest my sperm? Did I cry for my mommy and daddy and sister? Would it explain why, as a teenager, I was so scared all the time—scared of everything and anything? Would it explain why I hate doctors and dentists? Would it even explain why I eventually turned away from society, happily substituting humanity for Heroin?

"You're lucky we spotted you when we did," Sargent Applewhite told me when I had completely recovered from my Bantar sting and Scopolamine shot. "We caught a blip a few days ago but couldn't make a move while you were in Slag City. When we saw you had been cast out, we made a move."

"Where did all of those people come from?" I asked Applewhite about The Deinstitutionalized, the residents of The Great Bottom.

"They were test subjects. That's all anyone can really say. Top Brass still considers mass extermination unethical, so they've been left to their own devices for decades. They're not the only society of outcasts who have been banished. They aren't even the biggest group."

Outpost 10 was always buzzing. Drills, convoys, equipment testing.

"We have the ability to relocate the entire infrastructure of Washington D.C. all the way to an undisclosed location in Oregon," Applewhite explained. He gave me a tour of The Central Continental Corridor, carved by laser rock deflagration with walls that would never collapse or decay. It's the single greatest feat of engineering I'd ever seen. The section maintained at Outpost 10 was filled with imposing rows of war machines: Tanks, jets, helicopters, Jeeps, busses, and more.

Though my implant identified me as an authorized future colonist, granting me limited access to and autonomy within the facility, my arrival at Outpost 10 was nonetheless something Applewhite struggled to comprehend. Folks don't usually wander through unannounced.

"What were you doing in Slag City?" he asked during a casual, low-intensity interrogation. "Slag City" is what they called The Great Bottom. "Slags" were what they called the residents.

"I got lost... I was living in a runoff channel in Vegas, and I got lost."

"Did you come down before or after the Special Election?" Applewhite pressed.

"I don't remember any election."

Applewhite chose his words carefully. "Do you know who the President is?"

"I don't follow politics."

Applewhite erupted into a huge fit of laughter. "Oh man, you're in for a shock, my friend!"

After everything I'd been through, I was skeptical that anything happening above ground could legitimately shock me now—but I shouldn't have been.

"What's your current objective?"

"I... I told you, I got lost." I wasn't about to tell him the truth: That I was on a trek with my ghost buddy (who I can usually only see when I'm high) and that we're going to live with a caste of ancient, giants in a land without pain.

"You wouldn't mind taking a polygraph, would you?"

The soldiers assigned to Outpost 10 (established in 1959) were part of a legion known as The Defender Corps, chosen specifically for the Impending Aggregation. Recruits were subjected to an intensive regimen to prepare them for five to ten-year stints underground. They were also studying a concept known as "Thought Transference." Supposedly, practitioners could confuse and hypnotize their enemies on sight by articulating a series of vocal tones while simultaneous performing synchronized flagellations.

In order to become a Defender, soldiers were required to denounce all relationships with friends and family. Before being dispatched, they were "killed in action," meaning the Army faked their deaths and even held mock funerals for them. Becoming a Defender was a life-long commitment, one that Applewhite claimed his men accepted with great honor.

Drew told a different story: "They're part of the Phantom Army, a contingency of tens of thousands of supposedly dead soldiers. But it's not an honor, Sonny—they're dregs. These are the guys with serious psychological issues, problems that make them societal pariahs, but uniquely qualified for underground warfare. There's no place for them on the surface, so the government puts them to work in the Outposts."

There are only three reasons to bury something this deep, Drew reminded me: Because it's valuable, because it's secret, and because it's dangerous.

"They're Defenders, but they're also prisoners—and exiles," Drew warned me.

"All the timetables were accelerated after North Korea dropped the bomb on Japan. All the Government's top scientists now agree Day One is eminent," Applewhite explained. Day One is the name given to a theoretical point in time when all of mankind's previous history becomes inconsequential. It seemed to correspond, in an adjacent manner, to Archibald's Singularity and Drew's Greatest Conjunction Ever. And according to Applewhite, it had already begun.

"Everything's changing. There's a new President and everything's gone to shit. The borders have been closed and Martial Law was declared after 7/17."

"What's 7/17?" I asked.

"You have been under a rock!" Applewhite exclaimed. You remember 9/11, don't you? 7/17 made 9/11 look like a slow-news day. New York has been leveled. Los Angeles has been overrun by a new plague. Chicago and Atlanta are in chaos and the Federal Government has already relocated underground.

"It's going to get crowded down here," Applewhite continued in an ominous tone. "When we registered your tracker, we thought for a moment you were leading the first wave of new residents."

This reminded me of *The Mosquito Coast*, a movie I watched when I was a kid. It was about this dad who moved his family to the jungles of South America. And when his family said they wanted to go home, he told them that they couldn't because there had been a nuclear war and their home didn't exist anymore.

Is that what was happening now? Was Applewhite gaslighting me? And did any of it really matter anyway? Could anyone truly convince me that an Artificial Antichrist wasn't planning my eventual resurrection and endless torture?

Applewhite was the only resident of Outpost 10 who maintained contact with the Surface Command Center, he explained. He took the orders and passed them down among the ranks. His authority over the compound was absolute and unquestioned.

As an authorized future colonist, I was given a uniform and a single bunk in an otherwise uninhabited dormitory. Hundreds more empty beds were ready to accept future waves of underground refugees, those beginning their collective decent on or before Day One.

Not only was society crumbling quickly, but American's treaty with the Grays was also in shambles.

A new organization called The Aviary had been attempting to seize control of the Shadow Government. Their declaration of war stated: "We are dissatisfied with the handling of the UFO subject." They joined forces with the Ariel Phenomenon Research Organization (APRO) in 2003 becoming a legitimate potential usurper. The Defenders at Outpost 10 were preparing to eradicate the forces of The Aviary in subterranean combat, awaiting orders from high command—or a preemptive attack on their doorstep.

"We've been expecting our marching orders to arrive any day now," Applewhite confided. "Any day now... for years." A system of high-speed, vacuum-powered monorails were ready to shuttle Defenders into vast battlegrounds where cutting-edge weapons had already been installed. All manner of laser cannons and plasma rays and pew-pew-pew devices. These anticipated clashes will be explosive enough to register as major earthquakes above ground, Applewhite assured me. Still, when this war begins, only a select few surface dwellers will understand the true magnitude of the Earth's movement.

"What's the next part of our plan, Drew?" I finally inquired one night in my bunk.

"I'm sensing a manifestation of the Inverse Drake Equation," Drew muttered. "The Fourth Reich's been colluding with the Church of Euthanasia and the Knights of the Solar Temple. Plans for a final conflict were accelerated after the Treaty of Easter Island collapsed. The Greatest Conjunction Ever is at hand!"

I had no idea what he was on about, but one thing was certain: Nobody just walks out of Wonderland. There's no "Exit" sign in Outpost 10. Every day the tension rose, the walls seemed to close in, and the nameless, nebulous dread in my belly intensified into a searing ulcer.

"What's the next part of our plan, Drew?" I repeated.

"Hurry up and wait, Sonny. Hurry up and wait. Leave too soon and risk raising the alarm. Wait too long and miss our shot at Xanadu."

That night, Drew left on another scouting mission.

I bided me time, settling into my life as Outpost 10's first (and so far, only) civilian colonist. I went to the gym. I ate my rations. I read my daily intel reports. I watched dozens of instructional VHS videos produced by a contractor called ASync in 1994: Survival Techniques and Protocols.

I tried not to think about the girl in the desert, but of course I did.

CHAPTER
NINE

"Hey Sonny, did you know that President John Quincy Adams once funded an expedition to find life underground?"

We were still in a holding pattern, waiting for an unmistakable sign that it was time to make our next big move.

"The guy had a pet alligator, but that's a totally different story," Drew proceeded. "So, J.Q.A, the 6th President of the United States, he was an excellent diplomat. He was crisscrossing the globe on goodwill missions to Europe and South America—anywhere he could make a good impression and stack up allies should the British ever attempt to take back what they still referred to as 'The Colonies.'

"So, around this time, a guy named John Cleves Symmes, Jr. was crisscrossing the country looking for funding for an underground expedition. Symmes was one of the first scientist ambitious enough to follow the clues to 'Inner Earth' which he knew was a catacomb of layers, each with diverse ecosystems, each capable of supporting advanced civilizations. He'd been trekking from California to New Jersey, hitting up every institute of higher learning along the way for donations to fund his expedition.

"He didn't manage to rally much support in the way of money, but people were interested in his ideas, and he eventually went to Congress to pitch his expedition. While both houses scoffed, J.Q.A. was intrigued, especially by the idea of underground civilizations. Not only did he see potential for a military alliance, but he was also keen to investigate any trade potential. An underground society would have all kinds of exotic exports and would surely be interested in what a budding America could offer in return. So, after everyone else had passed, J.Q.A. decided to throw his support behind Symmes' venture and plans were set into motion. Under the President's guidance, a team would be assembled and dispatched to the North Pole within 2 years.

"It would have happened, too, except that J.Q.A. lost his re-election bid to Andrew Jackson. One of the first things that asshat did was axe funding to Symmes' expedition. Know why? Because Jackson was a fucking Flat Earther! He thought any expedition underground would end with explorers falling through the final inches of Earth and into infinity. Ridiculous! The man was completely unhinged. You know he shot someone, right?"

"You shot someone too, Drew."

"You got me there, Sonny."

The first blast rocked me completely out of my bunk.

"This is it, Sonny! This is the sign! It's showtime!"

Outpost 10 was then rocked by a second huge explosion. All power went out briefly, returning with a blaring siren and flashing red lights. Powdered concrete made the air look hazy.

Drew commanded me to brace myself.

Then he pushed me against the wall and began tearing into my abdomen with his boney fingers. I was too stunned to scream or thrash or protest in any manner. I just swallowed my pain and let Drew continue his mutilations. First, he created a deep, penetrating wound. Then he pulled the tear in my abdomen into a wide and gaping maw.

He wasn't much more than a skeleton, dripping viscera as his bones shed their last bits of decaying flesh. He no longer had lips or eyelids or a nose. He was naked and (of course) he stank.

"I'm coming in," he told me.

Drew proceeded to push his hands into my gushing torso. When both were wrist deep, he retracted my torn flesh to the maximum before sticking his head inside me. I fought back waves of terror, agony, and unconsciousness.

Once his arms and head were completely burrowed in my stomach, he began a desperate struggle to bury his shoulders. It was a reverse-birth scenario, and it was even more violent and messy than a grossly oversized baby's emergence from a tiny vagina.

Impossibly, he worked his shoulders into my torso. Bones (his and mine) were cracking, splintering, dripping marrow. His pelvis entered me with ease in comparison to his shoulders. He twisted around and drew his legs inside one after the other.

Once he was all the way in, he unfurled. I felt his legs run the length of my legs, as though he was putting me on like a pair of pants. His arms entered my arms like he was putting on a jacket. His head pushed through the narrow opening of my neck like a too-tight sweater—then popped into my head with a wet thump.

Our bodies were now both crowded into my meat-suit, superimposed into a single entity. It felt like I was being buried alive inside my own body.

"Is this what being possessed feels like?" I wondered.

The wound in my abdomen began to seal itself. First, the blood stopped gushing, then the flaps of distended flesh melted back together, leaving only a huge white scar where Drew had entered.

"Now" Drew said, "We're getting the fuck out of here!"

As terrifying and violating as it was having Drew usurp my body, it was also a tremendous relief. I ceded the position of control inside my brain, and he became the driver, the speaker, and the decider. For the first time since Drew dragged me underground, I could just sit back and watch the misadventures unfurl without being forced to choose my actions.

He was parasitic fungus to my nervous system, and I became his slave. No, it wasn't something I entered into willingly, but I was accustomed to having my freedom stolen and my body battled upon.

More explosions as Drew/I made a beeline into the fray. A soldier named Frost came running towards us: "Put this on!" he screamed, thrusting a gas mask into our hands.

"What's happening?" Drew/I asked.

"We're under attack! Sarg is dead! It's The Aviary! They've joined forces with the Reptilians!"

Someone else was squawking frantically into an intercom: "Battle stations... Heavy fire in Sector G... Scramble the drones..."

Drew/I put on the gas mask and pushed on. The man-made walls and corridors were crumbling, filling with smoke. We maneuvered deftly through thickening, toxic smoke. When we came under fire from an unseen intruder, Drew dodged bullets with supernatural swiftness. We came to an elevator and got inside, but as the doors closed, another explosion rocked us. The lift went black.

Even without light, Drew's dead eye had powers of perception. Super-vision, like infra-red capabilities displayed in bright computer animation. Drew/I examined our prison and quickly located an escape hatch in the ceiling. With the speed and dexterity of a puma, Drew/I exited the cramped compartment and climbed down the quacking shaft on a steel ladder.

Once at the bottom, Drew/I used some inhuman strength to pry the elevator doors open from the inside before sprinting out onto the intimidating expanse of The Central Continental Corridor. The Defenders had taken positions in a series of turrets. They fired red pulses in every direction, creating bone-cracking dissonance. Others were climbing into the cockpits of the F-16s and stealth bombers, getting ready to engage unseen attackers in the distant gloom.

"We're attempting to open The Threshold!" someone in a gas mask screamed at us. "Head to Sector J! You'll be safe inside The Backrooms!"

Drew and I both knew enough about The Backrooms to know that was the last place we'd ever want to be. They were the subject of multiple instructional videotapes whose contents Applewhite had insisted I familiarize myself with.

"In the likely event of a nuclear war, the entire US population will be transported to The Backrooms," the first video produced by ASync explained. Produced in 1994, it continued: "Project KV31 pertains to the study and development of the ASync Low Proximity Magnetic Distortion System© (model VI)."

Originally conceived with the seemingly innocuous intention of solving America's storage and residential housing needs, Project KV31 created a permanent entry point into The Backrooms, a portal known as "The Doorway" or "The Threshold".

"Under no circumstances should you enter The Threshold alone," another video advised. "Expeditions must be carried out in groups of three or more."

The instructional videos were stuffed with maps and diagrams. Later videos contained footage recorded within The Backrooms themselves—and it's some of the most terrifying shit Drew and I have ever seen.

What are The Backrooms? A definitive answer is difficult to parse, but it's a place that was discovered—not created. The Backrooms are an infinite assemblage of uniform yet random rooms and hallways. Though plans were made for residential occupation, the environment has an unabashedly corporate feel. For anyone who's worked a 9 to 5 job they hated, the Backrooms are pure Office Hell.

The wallpaper is a dingy yellow. The beige carpet is damp and musty. Illumination is provided by overhead florescent lights that buzz and hum incessantly and aggressively.

What's so scary about a bunch of rooms? For starters, you need to wear a full hazmat suite with an external breathing apparatus just to go inside. While people have been found "lost" and wandering through The Backrooms unprotected, they become hosts to an un-classified-bacterial strain that causes accelerated decomposition upon death.

Another scary thing about The Backrooms: They change. So even if you take detailed notes describing every turn you take, it could be impossible to return the way you came in. Expeditions carry a tracker device that leaves a trail of thick red tape reinforced with a plastic polymer. Even those aren't foolproof, though, and a carrier can find himself spontaneously "noclipped" into an unexplored section of The Backrooms.

So how big are The Backrooms? Now here's where things get really scary: While they aren't infinite, The Backrooms cover an estimated area of no less than nine million square miles—which is just insane! Getting lost in The Backrooms is likely a death sentence, although our relative lack of knowledge means that anything is possible.

ASync established control rooms within The Backrooms, along with motion-activated cameras. While the footage is hard to decipher one thing is certain: The Backrooms are inhabited. We don't know if the creatures who call this domain home are native or alien (or intraterrestrial)—but they are not from our dimension.

No, Drew and I would not be entering The Backrooms. Not today and never by our own volition.

"Carry on without us," Drew/I commanded. "Don't let those bastards through! Our entire future is in your hands!"

"Goodspeed!" the frantic soldier replied.

As he ran one way and we ran another, the fighting intensified. But I started to realize something troubling. While there was plenty of defensive firepower on display, I had yet to see a single intruder. Not a person or a machine that didn't already belong at Outpost 10. So, what were they firing at?

"Drew, are you thinking what I'm thinking?"

"They've all gone mad, Sonny! We're not under attack. They've lost their minds. We've got to get out of here before they initiate Sequence 74: Automatic Self Destruct. If we're not at least a mile away when they blow, we're dead."

Drew/I hopped into one of the Jeeps parked in a row against the east partition, keys ready in the ignition. The vehicle roared noisily to life when we turned it over. A moment later, we were speeding off into the sizable expanse, the sounds and fury of Outpost 10 beginning to fade.

Drew kept our foot on the gas and blasted us forward. Headlights illuminated the nothingness ahead until we turned down an intersecting corridor beginning a steep descent. Soon, we were in a tube that looked both natural and constructed. The walls were coated in some sort of crystalline material that sparkled under the headlights, creating beams of red and green and purple that refracted all around us.

Another tremendous blast hit us from behind. Everything shook with the intensity of a 9.9 on the Richter Scale. The Jeep lurched and rumbled as the corridor behind us began collapsing. A wave of intense, flesh singing heat was at our back, threatening to envelope us.

We shot out into a void. The ground beneath us disappeared and we arched downward into emptiness. Drew braced our body between the seat and the steering wheel as the Jeep hit freezing water. We had fallen through Wonderland's formidable infrastructure and plunged into Earth's top-most Inner Ocean.

The violent collision threw Drew/me from the vehicle and into a swirling bath of saltwater and bioluminescent algae. I had never learned to swim, but Drew had been an athlete and was still in complete control. The water churned and teemed with wide-eyed eels and mammoth tentacled cephalopods. Pods of plesiosaurs rocketed out from the water only to crash back into the sea, producing Himalayan-sized rouge waves.

After what felt like an hours-long struggle against an oppressive undertow, Drew/I finally pulled ourselves from the frigid drink and onto a sandy green embankment.

"This is as good a time as any for you to pass out, Sonny."

I awoke in a chilly, domed chamber. It was like being inside a stone igloo. Drew had separated us into individuals again—a process I was happy to have slept through. He had collected heaps of dried moss, which he'd heaped over my body in order to stave off hypothermia. There wasn't any fire, but there was still illumination, a dim iridescence I couldn't explain, as nothing seemed to be overtly glowing or shining. Everything looked natural—except for the red door.

I mean, it looked like it was in an eons-old lava bubble, a place no human eyes had ever seen. But there it was, a wooden door. The red paint looked freshly lacquered and the knob was brilliant brass without a hint of rust or oxidation. I wondered what was behind it with enchantment and gut-churning trepidation.

"Where are we?" I asked my ghost buddy when my voice returned.

"We're not in Wonderland anymore," Drew informed me—as if it wasn't obvious.

"What happened?"

"You saw it just like I did: They all went crazy. They blew themselves up."

"What is this place?" I inquired, looking sheepishly at the door.

"Just a stopover. We're close Sonny—really close. But there's something you have to do first."

"What's that?"

Drew smiled: "You have to snort some Alien Dust—and then you have to talk to Eve."

"I don't understand anything you just said to me," was my reply, but Drew just pointed at the door implying I had to see for myself.

The knob turned with a click and the door swung open, as if pulled by a sudden change in air pressure. It was pitch black for a moment, dark and foreboding, but Drew wouldn't allow me to retreat. As he pushed me inside and the red door swung shut again with a heavy, resonating slam.

When my eyes adjusted to the darkness I was utterly stunned. I expected to find myself in immediate peril, possibly surrounded by unknown creatures. At the very least, I expected to find something disgusting and deplorable.

Instead, it was a luxurious lobby, something you'd expect in an expensive hunting lodge. There were couches and armchairs. The walls were made of expensive oak paneling and 19th Century oil paintings adorned the walls. In the center of the room, a comfortable chair was set up in front of a 1960s era television set. There was a small end table beside the chair with several objects on it. A disembodied hiss seemed to beckon me to "Sit."

I did and I couldn't remember the last time I'd felt so comfortable. An ottoman slid out from under the chair, allowing me to kick my legs up like a king.

The end table to my right had a remote for the TV on it. It was one of those ancient monstrosities the size of a small book with 4 huge buttons that required a bit of effort to depress. Beside the remote was a small round mirror. On top of the mirror was a straw and four lines of pristine white powder. My heart began racing at the mere sight.

"Snort Me" a hand-written note invited.

"Twist my arm," I joked aloud to the empty room. Hands trembling with excitement, I took the straw and the mirror and greedily inhaled my first line.

I was on a path towards the Warm Oblivion, a state of existence I'd practically given up on ever experiencing again. No, the powder wasn't Heroin. It was what Drew had previously referred to as Alien Dust, a compound created in the laboratory of a now-decommissioned MK Ultra facility.

Experimentations had revealed the compound effected internal human vibration, allowing those under its influence to contact beings in other dimensions and maybe even alternate realities.

The second line put me in a state of superb enjoyment. There were all the hallmarks of the Warm Oblivion, but none of the oppressive fog. If anything, two lines of Alien Dust made me feel focused, like years of cobwebs had been spontaneously swept from my brain, allowing a level of clarity I didn't know existed (or had forgotten).

When I hit line number three, I thought I'd found Nirvana. Colors jumped and flickered as my brain fired neurons that had been dormant all my life, causing complex and euphoric epiphanies. I was also overcome by a powerful sensation of pure, unadulterated love. Nothing bothered me: Not Hauptnadle's molestations or Archibald's manipulations. The Bantar's sting was a distant memory, as was Thaddaeus.

I insufflated the fourth and final line with triumph. Leaning back into the velvet chair, my individual cells somersaulted onto previously unknown echelon of pleasure.

The TV turned on all by itself as I sat transfixed. At first, there was nothing but static, a black and white snowstorm with patterns emerging and drowning. Eventually, the static cleared, and I found myself looking into the sparkling blue eyes of a female entity.

Entity?

Something about her immediately struck me as extraterrestrial (or at the very least, intraterrestrial), specifically her lack of hair and a nose. Her skin was as pale as a piece of paper.

Her name was Eve, and she was an ambassador from another state of existence. The impending Conjunction threatened to obliterate the walls between our dimensions, meaning the potential existed for our lives to become intertwined.

Eve told me that Drew and I needed to hurry if we intended to make it to Xanadu in time. She promised to give me the keys we needed. She also said she would answer any of my most burning questions. But first, I had to do something for her.

"What happened to the girl in the desert?" she inquired, though the tone of her voice made it clear she already knew.

It wasn't about me conveying information she wasn't aware of. No, it was time for me to own up, to unlock the vault I'd buried my memories inside of. Merely hesitating exasperated the dangerous conundrum I was in. If I didn't admit to everything, my journey would end immediately—Drew's too.

I opened the vault.

"I came to Las Vegas for a bachelor party. Jeremy was marrying my sister, Gina. Before we flew out, she pulled me aside and made me promise that, if Jeremy did anything unbecoming of a future husband and father, I'd tell her. She was afraid he was going to fuck a stripper or something. Even though it would be totally out of character, she never trusted Jeremy's brothers, Falcon and Mick—and she was right not to. Those two were terrible and they had a way of making Jeremy do things he would never do otherwise."

It might seem like I'm stalling, but I'm not. This is important.

"On our first night in Vegas, they hired two strippers to entertain the bachelor and his guests. These two tweaked out teenagers were naked within five minutes of arriving, and the whole room was hooting and hollering. Then, they pulled all of Jeremy's clothes off and—they just started fucking him right there on the sofa, in front of everybody.

"As I got up to leave, Falcon pushed me up against a wall and was like, 'Look, I know he's marrying your sister and it's important for you to be the protective "big brother," but if you breathe a word of this to Gina, I'll cut your fucking balls off. Don't be a fucking pussy. Let Jeremy have his fun and keep your fucking mouth shut.'"

It doesn't seem like much. Not compared to facing down demons or traversing jagged chasms—but this shit was hard for me...

"The thought of going home again, of looking into Gina's eyes and either breaking her heart or lying to her face, was more than I could handle. So, I didn't... I didn't go home again. I emptied my bank account, pawned my watch and electronics, and went on my bender. Of course, I was already familiar with drugs, you know, but this time, it was anything goes and the more the merrier. When I finally met Heroin, it was like, everything in my life made sense—like every misstep I'd taken in my pathetic life had brought me to her Queendom, and I was desperately in love.

"I met Melissa downtown one night," I continued confessing to Eve, "when we were both desperate to find Thaddaeus. After we scored, we decided to hole up in a cheap motel and shot for days."

I don't know what she saw in me, but she was awesome—amazing. Emo, Goth, a sinister Suicide Girl. We became inseparable... partners in crime and in Oblivion.

I never learned what circumstances had brought her to Las Vegas because I didn't ask. It didn't matter. It was as though neither of us had lived before we became junkies, and nothing mattered beyond our immediate need to fly. It's not that I didn't love her. It's just that I didn't love her as much as I loved Heroin.

Love and Heroin is a great combination. But it's not as good as Heroin and Heroin.

"We killed a John!" I blurted out. "We were going to rob him. I was hiding in the closet with a switchblade. He started strangling her, so I busted out and started stabbing. And once she regained her composure, she grabbed her switchblade and we both kept stabbing and stabbing..."

Eve was silent yet demanded more details with a commanding gaze that probed my most fractured recesses. The details were not for her pleasure, they were for my punishment.

"When he was dead, we took all the money from his wallet and took the rental car he'd left in the motel parking lot. We found Thaddaeus and bought so much Heroin. We'd never made such a big score in a single day, and we felt like royalty. We couldn't go back to the motel because we were certain the cleaning crew had already discovered the body in the bathtub. We were afraid the cops would be looking for us, or that there was an alert out for the rental car.

"We decided to buy a sleeping bag and head out into the desert. We imagined finding a quiet mesa or an oasis. Someplace where we could spend hours at peace in the Warm Oblivion. We didn't have any plans for what would come next because—I think because we knew this was the end. We usually rationed our Heroin to keep from running out too quickly, but there was no need this time. Our wad was the size of a golf ball! She shot me first and it was absolute bliss. Then she said, 'My turn'."

I hesitated. A high-pitched whining began to permeate the room. "Continue," Eve commanded.

"I gave her the biggest shot of her life. I watched her face light up and she burst into a huge smile. She looked me right in the eyes and slowly exhaled for the last time. Her eyes never closed again and she never broke her smile."

"It was an accident?" Eve pressed.

"I did it on purpose," I confessed. "I killed her so I could have all the rest of the Heroin for myself."

After the most beautiful sunset I'd ever seen, I wrapped Melissa's body in the sleeping bag and put her in the back of the stolen rental car. I ignited the gas tank and managed to sprint for about three hundred yards before it blew up. I hitched a ride back to Las Vegas the next morning and moved into the tunnels the next day. The rest, you already know.

I was a blathering wretch. It was everything I had refused to lay bare, everything I had hoped to burry beneath mountains of junk. The truth that sent me recoiling backwards into one inescapable hole after another.

Eve seemed neither impressed nor upset at my reveal. She offered neither reassurance nor condemnation. She merely processed the information. Then, it was my turn to sit and listen. I didn't even have to ask my question. She knew what I wanted—and she knew it would devastate me.

"There are such mysteries in your world simply waiting to be discovered," Eve pontificated. "Universal truths staring you all in the face. Those who merely scratch the surface are often condemned as madmen. They're labeled as traitors and heretics. Repeating toxic cycles, imploding in on yourselves. Such convoluted self-obsession—and at the cost of unimaginable treasures. Equating yourselves with Gods while lacking the reasoning capabilities of most insects. A race of wasted potential, a self-consuming cancer that eats itself while attacking innocents. Like a newborn unable to crawl from his own afterbirth—abandoned. Waiting to be saved while embracing... oblivion."

The effects of Alien Dust wear off after about an hour.

This Lynchian ritual completed, I was banished from Eve's presence and returned to the stone antechamber on the other side of the red door. Drew was waiting impatiently.

"You know what we have to do," he said. It wasn't a question, rather a statement of fact.

"Yes," I replied.

"You have the key?"

"We both do."

Our tickets to Xanadu came in the form of a leap of faith. Eve had revealed the location of an abyss, something the likes of which we couldn't fathom. She didn't give us directions on a map. Instead, she transmitted the data on an ethereal and cellular level. Like boats to a beacon, like moths to a flame, we'd be drawn to the precipice like swallows coming home to Capistrano.

And so began the last great leg of our impossible adventure.

We walked. We walked for hours, days, and weeks (and probably years). We walked North, South, East, and West—but always down. Down rock faces more treacherous than Half-Dome. Down staircases that plunged into darkness without walls or a ceiling, plummeting to depths so extreme it felt like walking upside-down in a Maurits Cornelis Escher picture. We even went down miles-long escalators, clearly built by man except that their immensity and geography made that possibility impossible. Who then built these hallways, these courtyards—this labyrinth?

Past cave paintings and billboards from Martian skyscrapers we walked, past rocks and minerals and discarded bits of future technologies we walked. We met Frodo, Gollum, and experienced all the horrors of Mordor. We met Morlocks, Sasquatch, and Crab People. We crossed paths with Alice on her way back through the Lookingglass. We saw creatures that would have driven H.P. Lovecraft mad, faces that would make Cthulhu wretch. We dodged albino dinosaurs, swam freezing lakes, traversed icy tundra, and arid deserts. We walked into the 4th and 5th and 6th dimensions and then all the way back again.

"So, are you a ghost or a zombie?" I asked Drew one day when I figured it was way past time to set the record straight. He was barely half a skeleton now.

"I think the most accurate term for me is Revenant, someone who returns from death. I'm not a zombie because I'm not actually physical. Still, my ethereal form is tied to my corporal body."

"So, basically, you're the main character's best friend in *An American Werewolf in London*."

"Basically." Drew conceded.

But our small talk had long since evaporated by the time we arrived at Eve's pre-ordained destination. So much so that Drew hardly allowed for a moment of contemplation, reflection, or commemoration. He grabbed me around the waist and pushed us both tumbling over the precipice.

Drew and I were falling through pitch blackness with only the rush of air to indicate which end was up. Falling became a sensation of weightlessness—an oblivion in and of itself. Eventually, all sound disappeared, and it was like floating through outer space.

CHAPTER
TEN

"In 2002, a special unit of American soldiers serving in Afghanistan killed a 13-foot, redheaded giant that emerged from a cave in Kandahar."

"Fuck you, Drew."

"It's true, Sonny. Just Google 'The Kandahar Giant'." (Like, I somehow had access to the internet from inside my egg!)

"No, fuck you. I'm done."

"What's up your ass?"

"It's just pointless. It's meaningless. You know what, Drew? You fell down a hole long before we went underground. You drank the fucking Kool-Aid and jumped down an internet rabbit-hole and now your just another pathetic conspiracy theorist."

I expected a witty, scathing retort—but nothing. So, I leaned in.

"When you start giving credence to Nazi Occultists and Illuminati Slave Drivers, well, you're bound to end up in a Deep Underground Military Base. Because—aliens! No job, no family, no plans for the future—a future that doesn't end in a war with robots. Your life doesn't make sense, Drew. Someone as smart, savvy, and healthy as you should never have been living the tunnel life. A fuck-up like me, sure, that makes sense, but not someone like you, Drew. But you found yourself living in a tunnel and instead of figuring out whatever is inside you that brought you there, you created this fantasy where you're exactly where you're supposed to be. You concocted these earth-shaking ramifications. You created this unifying theory that connected it all. You put in all this effort, wasted these countless hours, because it was easier than turning your critical eye inside."

"But we actually made it, Sonny," Drew finally replied.

Of course he was right, in this case. But I was too.

You could go to any random spot-on Google Maps, dig straight down for decades and never find a damn thing—or you could find something bound to upend the universe just 20 meters deep.

People can't fathom what they can't see, and that's why we as a species spend trillions flinging junk into space instead of exploring our own oceans. Somehow, being able to see the dim glow of a long-dead star, billions of light-years away, is more relevant than the living gods and monster swimming the same oceans our own biological ancestors crawled out of.

And what is there at the top of Mount Everest besides garbage and corpses and an atmosphere so thin it will kill you? Nothing! Now, what's at the bottom of the Mariana Trench? Life! Treasure! Infinity! And the Mariana Trench is only seven miles deep. So, what can you find seven miles below that? Or 100 miles below? 1,000 miles below?

You know what's ironic? Even if we had the technology to build spaceships, we wouldn't find anything out there in space. And it's not because space is dead (even though most of the aliens are), it's just that there's nothing more wonderous out there than what you can find right here—underwater or underground. It's more than just awe-inspiring or mind-boggling—it's everything.

It's not just a source of wonder. It's a potential salvation. The answer to pollution, overpopulation, disease—even unhappiness. Of course, salvation comes at a price, and the road is paved with un-plumbed perils.

My particular journey, my horrors, represent just a fraction of what thrives and terrifies in the crust beneath us.

I'd always loathed insects—but they're what saved my life.

The final hole I'd fallen down (my leap of faith) wasn't empty space. Millions of spider-subspecies had ballooned down over countless millennia, creating gossamer netting that tore as I dropped through it. But there was more than web. Pre-historic bees built hives in the crevices, everything dripping a viscus byproduct. Transparent centipedes the size of freight trains molted, casting their husks as they grew at alarming speeds. Small mammals and reptiles who'd stumbled into this pit were trapped and devoured, but their hair and bones remained.

All of this waste and more combined with the organic cast off a billion undocumented, unnamed insects, sizes ranging from pubic lice to dolphins, anything that had passed through this pit by design or happenstance, through cyclical migrations that coincided with interplanetary alignments or by dumb luck. They'd all left bits of themselves, from grains of fecal waste to all manner of milks and secretions from swarms of larva and quivering egg sacks. Mana from Heaven.

And it was this semi-solid vector jetsam that surrounded me as I fell much farther than almost any man before me. First like sour wisps of cotton candy before the larger chunks of skin, broken legs, wings, and antennae accumulated evenly as I spun through darkness. The debris formed into a pulpy mush. Air pressure and gravity hardened the layers.

I fell through several unique atmospheres, detecting changes in humidity and heat, melding with the cooling rush of wind from beneath me. This bizarre, random process equaled perfection in the form of life-saving symmetry.

I was in the core of what must have looked like a giant hairy ovum, debris trailing like tentacles—like the putrid tail of a vomitous comet. The pit began to curve, ever so slightly at first, allowing my protective casing to slow as it ricocheted before eventually, shooting out like a pinball.

I was blasted into a vast cavern, landing on a black sandy beach on the edge of a river. Miles off a dwarf volcano painted the hot atmosphere in purples and crimsons. Soon, I heard hands and tools cracking the shell, breaking through layers, digging me out—and I waited with a mix of desperation and dread. Like everything else about my unfurling adventure, I expected to go from the frying pan into the fryer. I was right of course. I was wiser now than I was when I first left Las Vegas under Thaddaeus's gun.

And now I know everything because I've eaten the Sacred Moss.

The Grim Finger Clanspeople are a race of true troglodytes who have been living underground for over forty-thousand years. They evolved past the need for language long ago.

The Sacred Moss grows along the walls of caverns below a certain depth. It's an incredibly bitter, black substance that burns the nose and throat on the way down. Side effects include extreme nausea and migraines.

Once digested, however, the Sacred Moss allows for telepathic communication with those also under its influence. The Grim Finger Chief fed me the Sacred Moss when I proved to him that I was both intelligent and extremely submissive.

I survived a plane crash when I was five years old: PSA Flight 1777. It's not something I like to talk about, mostly because I don't remember. My parents were divorced so, every summer, I'd fly back and forth between Sacramento and San Diego, splitting my vacations equally. I was asleep when the plane landed, skidded off the runway, and burst into flames. Ironically, being asleep saved my life because my body was relaxed and limp. My entire row of seats was dislodged and tossed hundreds of yards away from the explosive inferno. The people on each side of me, strangers, both died—impaled by mangled debris as the plane shattered and cartwheeled. I was the sole survivor. My mom told me it was a miracle, that God himself must have protected me from an otherwise un-survivable scenario. "You've been chosen," she told me, would tell me, every day. Until it drove me crazy.

After nodding off in a shooting gallery a couple of years ago, I woke up to find someone had tattooed the letters "H-E-L-L" across the knuckles on my left hand. Some prankster's idea of a laugh-riot, I supposed. Truth is, I couldn't have cared less.

The tribe knew I was coming. Falling and accumulating the mass of my parachute-egg caused a whistling noise to echo throughout the cavern below—an audio harbinger announcing my impending arrival.

The exit of the seemingly bottomless pit is a favorite hunting ground for the Grim Finger Clanspeople, as meaty morsels are delivered in an incapacitated form that eliminates the inherent dangers of killing startled prey. It's like ordering your meat from your local grocer and having it arrive nicely wrapped in thick white paper. They eagerly chipped away at my sticky, milky layers until they unwrapped me from the core, coated in slime and crawling with larva. Everything hurt and I'd never been more terrified.

I was screaming for Drew without even knowing it. Like a newborn infant clearing its lungs. I bellowed like these were my very first gulps of air. I hollered like I was expelling soot and fire from my core. This amused the tribe. They began imitating me, filling the cavern with whoops and shrieks that combined into an a-melodic concerto.

Like all animals that fell from above, The Grim Finger Clanspeople considered me merely meat. They bound my arms and legs. They gagged me by placing a smooth rock in my mouth and gluing my lips together with a fatty tincture. The march back to their city took hours, so I drifted in and out of consciousness. When I was unable to walk and too heavy to drag, I was hoisted onto the back of a work-animal, something the size of a mule with the look and feel of a naked rat.

"Welcome to Xanadu, Sonny."

It was Drew's voice in my head. I slowly opened my eyes, hoping to take in the glorious paradise I'd been promised. Instead, I beheld an unholy environment that could only exist on a conceptual, metaphysical level deeper than Hell.

This city, while objectively beautiful, was disgusting in equal measure. Like the artwork of Hieronymus Bosch combined with an H.R. Giger nightmare. The Grim Finger Clanspeople resided in domiciles constructed from giant hollowed-out mushrooms, fortified with mud and natural glass. Temples and arenas seemed to have emerged from the ground itself, spirals stabbing upwards, circled by winged serpents. The streets of this city had an organic, semi-metallic composition. The surface was dotted with holes and vents that blasted periodic gusts of blistering humidity, as if the city itself was breathing. I was brought

into a grand communal dining area where they planned to prepare me
for immediate ritualistic consumption.

I wasn't the first surface dweller to fall into the pit. Strays from The
Great Bottom tumbled down at semi-regular intervals. They figured I
was just another paint-eater: tasty meat for the fires, sturdy bones for
weapons and jewelry.

The Grim Finger Clanspeople still look somewhat human because
they are human. Cave dwellers who went deeper while other emerged
into the sunlight. They had lived generations in pitch blackness before
arriving in caverns illuminated by scalding vents and glistening mi-
crobes. They found their Jerusalem, their Holy Land, the place Drew
called Xanadu, after thousands of years crossing underwater oceans,
annihilating predatory species, fracturing into subtribes, and praying
to the God of Meat.

They weren't giants like Drew hypothesized, but they were taller
than most men. Their skin was pale to the point of translucence, with
red, purple, and blue veins running like highways across their extremities—their abnormally long extremities. A Grim Finger Clansperson
can rest his or her fingertips on the ground without kneeling or bend-
ing down in the slightest. They wear leathered animal skins around
their bellies and their genitals. Their lips and teeth are permanently
stained black from suckling Sacred Moss. Their eyes were pure white
sclera without a trace of iris.

They were both primitive and transcendent, devoid of technologies
and ruled by principals unlocked from reptile brainstems. The dis-
covery of the Sacred Moss eliminated the need for language, uniting
the entire race on a cerebral level. The Sacred Moss also eliminated
the need for written records, instead creating a cache of knowledge
exponentially more illuminating than the Library of Alexandrea, an
unabridged information depository available to all. A mouthful of
Moss grants admission.

My mom had me involuntarily committed to a psychiatric facility
when I was fifteen. She told doctors and police that I was a danger to
myself and others. She suspected I was in the throes of some insidious

drug addiction. Ironically, the hospital's where I got my first taste of the really good shit. Regular cocktails of tranquilizers and opioids interspersed with group therapy and individual torture sessions. It's also where I lost my virginity.

Other physiological features that would immediately differentiate a Grim Finger Clansperson from a surface dweller include elongated skulls and boney protrusions along their spines. They'd also developed a sixth toe, one that hooked down from just above the heel, allowing them to transverse subterranean extremes, from slippery slopes to razor sharp shards of lava-rock and quarts with dexterity. They spread colorful clays into their hair creating thick chunks that were sculpted into spikes, locks, and swirls. They were beautiful and disgusting.

In preparation for the feast, I had been crucified. The skin on my left leg had been completely peeled off. The pain equaled my terror. I was surrounded by a crew of chefs and butchers. I could hear and smell the strips of my skin sizzling on hot rock stovetops like bacon. Appetizers for the main course.

As was tradition, The Grim Finger Chief had an extremely specific role to play in my ritual slaughter. Thankfully, he recognized that I was an unusual specimen. As he approached with an organ extraction device, I looked into his eyes and pleaded. I said "Please" so many times the word lost meaning. The very letters decomposed into a meaningless sludge of indecipherable screeching.

He gave me a heavy slap to shut me up. I quieted my whimpering, but continued to look into his blank white eyes, silently pleading with all my might, searching for mercy. He paused for several intense moments before commanding a couple of his underlings to cut me down. Another crammed a fistful of sour Sacred Moss into my mouth. I thrashed as the psychotropic pulp seared its way down my esophagus. The bitter mass hit my stomach acids, causing an instant chain-reaction that blasted outward from my core like a grenade.

"Kneel before your Savior, slag!"

I couldn't tell who gave the command to me because no one's mouth had moved. The words were spoken directly into my brain.

I stumbled towards the Chief, my left leg almost giving out as hot dust clung to my flayed flesh. I crumpled before him and erupted into gratitude.

"Thank you thank you thank you thank you..." I emoted without words. And the Chief, along with everyone else in the immediate vicinity, heard me. They enjoyed my subservience. They were impressed by my desire to live.

"You come from above," the Chief stated. It wasn't a question that required an answer. It was proof that my mind was now an open book for he and all The Grim Finger Clanspeople to read. They took my limited knowledge, added it to their vast information depository, and explained the universe in terms I could understand.

"That world is above gone," he told me. "Fire from the sky. Demigods in the halls of power. Petty diseases combining into unprecedented pandemics. The Greatest Conjunction Ever is at hand, and only those at peace with God will survive to sleep again."

"I'm at peace with God," I assured the Chief who responded with laughter and condemnation.

"It's not for you to declare. God decides if peace shall be granted."

I clasped my hands and begged, "God grant me peace... please God, grant me peace..."

The Chief kicked me and replied, "We don't pray. We speak to God face-to-face. Will you oblige?"

Was this what Drew had been talking about the whole time? Was Xanadu, in fact, not a place, but an experience—the experience of meeting God?

"Yes," I proclaimed with conviction. "I'm ready to speak to God—face-to-face."

The privilege came with a heavy price: A ritual to prepare me for my meeting would also serve as a rite of acceptance (should I survive).

There are no days in The Grim Finger Clanspeople's city, only endless hours of shifting illuminations: Red, Purple, Green, and Foggy. I spent these cycles enduring complicated rounds of bodily mutilations, with intricate patterns carved into my remaining skin. I was coated in clays and salves concocted from the eyes of reptiles and organs of unclassified mammals. They put me into a ceramic vessel and filled it with a near boiling mixture of wax and oil, only allowing me to breathe through tubes forced down my nostrils. I was sealed into a box with billions of larval arachnids who feasted on the puss that gushed from my wounds. I was cleaned in a bubbling pool of sulfur water and hung upside down by my ankles until blood spewed from my nose like a gusher.

No, they weren't trying to kill me or merely torture me. If that had been the case, I'd have known it. The Sacred Moss prevented lies. The ritual was brutal—but it was pure.

Back in Vegas, people always used to comment on how much Drew and I looked alike. "You guys could be twins!" I didn't see it. Drew had an aura of power and health. My aura was dull yellow and gray, like earwax.

Drew was now just a floating skull with red, glowing eyes. I sometimes had to laugh when I saw him, because he reminded me of something I might have put on my shelf in college—next to my lava lamp! He'd show up, say something condescending like, "Hang in there, Sonny!" before flying around in inverted figure-eights. Believe me, if they ever made this into a movie, it'll look ridiculous.

I was sealed into a cold chamber with a screeching earth-monkey and a gargantuan mantis. "Kill them both and eat them both," the Chief instructed, "And then it will be time for you to meet God."

The mantis was easy to kill. The monkey—not so much. And not just because it was stronger than me, but because of how it pleaded for its life. Not with words, not with telepathy, but with pitiful sobs that sounded like a teenage girl weeping. I wasn't hungry, but I gorged myself, consuming bones and hair and everything.

I didn't have to tell the Chief when I was finished because he already knew. The chamber was unsealed and he stood in the opening, a great white light behind him.

"It's time."

I was slathered with fresh batches of colored clay and adorned in decorative leathers and bones. The Chief led me towards the Great Doorway, behind which I would meet my maker. Legions of Grim Finger Clanspeople followed me, chanting beautiful, haunting hymns telepathically. "We made it Drew," I muttered, tears of joy flowing.

"I knew you could do it Sonny. I always believed in you!" cheered Drew as he flew above the celebratory crowds that had gathered.

The Great Doorway was guarded by The Processor, a human-pachyderm hybrid whose species had been domesticated by The Grim Finger Clanspeople millennia prior. He stood like a man but looked more like an elephant. He had slippery, gray skin like a dolphin. He had long fingers, each capped with a sharp nail that dripped a honey-colored liquid. He was there to prepare my mind and body for my meeting with God, a penultimate component of the ceremony.

The Processor touched my arm and delivered a dose of his nectar into my bloodstream. Boom: My pupils turned to pinpricks. My heart raced I realized I really was home.

I was swimming in the glistening pools of the Warm Oblivion, diving deeper than I ever dreamed possible.

The Great Doorway opened, and I was ushered into the royal antechamber. It slammed shut with an echoing thump that resonated throughout my entire body and, probably, the entire world. This was the Waiting Room, and I was ready to meet God.

Delighted with anticipation, I was cast into a tempest of memories: The shootout with Thesaurus, Drew's murder at the hands of the hideous codger, the tortures of Hauptnadle and his acolytes, the indoctrination of Archibald and Dr. Sasha, the prison of Forbidden Knowledge, the threat of the Basilisk, the realm of SPC-087, my short-lived partnership with The Junk Man, my humiliations on The Great Bottom, the fever-inducing venom of the Bantar, The Outpost and its motley crew, my face-to-face communion with an entity named Eve—all of it. Everything.

The most beautiful angelic voices began to sing.

God will see me now.

CHAPTER
ELEVEN

MY PATH TO THE bottom was random but deliberate, like a metal marble, reacting only to gravity, rolling through an elaborate series of grooves and shoots, setting off handguns, snapping strings, lighting candles, and toppling dominos, before triggering a mousetrap (or making toast).

Whether it was a path of deliberate design or a random convergence of circumstance akin to a cartoon fiasco is open to debate. Still, if I had veered from my descent in the slightest, changed direction by mere degrees, hesitated moments, or taken one of innumerable wrong turns, I never would have made it. I'm like the survivor of a tsunami who slept through the entire ordeal who wakes up floating on a calm ocean, still in bed while thousands of others were crushed and drowned or trampled.

Of course, I hadn't slept through anything. I'd been churned in the crushing convergence of events and individuals that turned Drew into chum. From the moment Thaddaeus snapped me out of the Warm Oblivion with a hail of gunfire, I'd swirled into one hellish eddy after another.

Sleep was either a luxury, something compulsory forced by chemicals, or the result of incomprehensible agony. Sleep was paradise denied by demons like Hauptnadle or enforced by medically induced comas. How long has it been since I'd last enjoyed the slightest hint of blissful unconsciousness—the slumber of the innocent? No way of knowing. No way to measure hours or days until I fine-tune my senses to the gossamer pull of the Moon and Betelgeuse. No, I hadn't

slept through any of the metaphorical or allegorical tidal waves that
forced me down a sinkhole on an unfathomable destination, deeper
than Hell.

Or had I?

I remembered that time I thought I woke up. Felt the Sun shining
on my face, blissfully burning my retina back to life. I remembered
that conversation I had with Drew, dead Drew, about *Jacob's Ladder*.
I remembered all those times I slammed dirty Heroin when Drew was
nowhere in sight, almost daring him to find me in time. He always
did. It was almost uncanny. It was almost like I couldn't escape him;
couldn't keep a secret he wouldn't know about.

Almost like he was a projection of myself, my survival mode manifested, lurking in the shadows until needed. Always there to protect
me as I slept—the man I never was with the bravery I could never
muster. My personal Tyler Durden willing to do the dirty work when
I couldn't (or wouldn't).

Mine was a one in a billion convergence of dumb luck and cosmic
conjunctions, but my path isn't the only one that leads to Xanadu.
There are the massive openings at the North and South Poles (the
worst kept of the world's most dangerous secrets), and dozens of
others—at least. The desert around Las Vegas, obviously, but also the
caves of Peru and the sarcophagi of Hungry were explorers unearthed
the remains of nine-foot, Aryan giants with orange hair.

Besides the physical, literal paths, there are the metaphysical door-
ways that lead to God's antechamber. The yogis of India and the
meditating Buddhist monks of China have found passage without
ever moving a muscle. Those born as astral projectors as well as those
trained in remote viewing have, unwittingly, seen more than they
might have bargained for. There are wormholes, both naturally occurring and mechanically harnessed, that could have made my arduous,
miserable, magical tragic trek instantaneous.

But if a million people made this place their destination, maybe four
would actually get here. The last time someone from the surface got

half this deep (and lived more than the few moments necessary for butchery) was about twelve-thousand years ago.

I've seen God. There is no room for misinterpretation.

If you think you can't imagine—keep doubting.

I'd sooner shoot myself in the head than inflict it on anyone. It's not my fault if you're hearing this, reading this. I warned you. Explicitly. The plus side is you aren't damned like I am—not yet at least. I could never convey this Forbidden Knowledge, not with every word of every language and ten thousand years at my disposal.

When the curtain fell and the door swung opened, I was instantly fractured at a metaphysical and molecular level. I was fractured between what I had assumed was the present and the infinity of temporal nuances connecting knowledge stored in the lizard brain with the new testaments of yet unborn omniscient machinery.

I was fractured between what I assumed was my personal identity and the consciousness of every other human, subhuman, and superhuman. My name is Sonny, but I'm Drew. I'm Thaddaeus, Hauptnadle, and Archibald. My name is Sonny but I am the Junk Man, the Demon of Montauk, and every soul imprisoned in the SCP containment facility. My name is Sonny, but I am Dr. Sasha, the jester-priest with eyeballs hanging from his headdress, the insidious Bantar dripping venom. My name is Sonny, but I am every soldier stationed at every deep underground military base in America, the legislators empowering the death squads, the powers that be keeping even the most free-spirited bohemian chained and oppressed. I am the army of goblins you falsely assumed came from another planet.

My name is Sonny, but I am Mother Horse Eyes, the Dali Lama, and every refugee banished to the Backrooms. My name is Sonny, but my name is impossible to pronounce in the vast continuum of microcosms and macroverses. My name is the laughter of children, the battle cry of the bloodthirsty, and the prattle of the madmen.

Looking at the face of God brings a crush of epiphanies and awakenings, along with infinite death and never-ending rebirth. Looking at the face of God brings knowledge of The Elders. It unlocks the secrets of primordial ooze, revealing the recipes for natural selection and cosmic enslavement. The basics of facial communication and the most advanced and convoluted computer programs are all utterances of a single vocabulary.

Looking at the face of God causes a collision of science and religion, creates a combustible concoction unleashing Big Bangs in brains, allowing connections to shadow people and insect statisticians, the beings living mute and invisible behind the cloak of unabsorbed DMT. Looking into the face of God crushes fear of pain, the finality of decay, and the immense sorrow of breathing.

The breath of God is hot and caustic, poisonous and delicious, sober and intoxicating. The breath of God conjures images of the pulsating intergalactic vagina, rivers of melted flesh and fetuses, and the dizzying geometry of Ezekiel's Wheel. The breath of God brings Pi full circle, puts Infinity into a nutshell, obliterating the objectivity of physical mass and electrical voltage. The breath of God burns intense like the gases of a supernova while delivering a chill below absolute zero, indescribable joys and unfathomable dread.

When God speaks, each immaculate syllable leaves an indelible mark. He chose the voice of Drew to deliver his loving brutality, this monsoon of blisters and breakthroughs, world-building and immeasurable cataclysms.

"They're all afraid to die, Sonny. They all want to live forever. They think immortality is a reward or a blessing. It isn't Sonny. It's a curse. Experience this, a mere sliver of the disembodied infinity: A googolplex of endless seconds to ponder a single flickering existence. Alone with regret, heartbreak, and guilt—forever. There is no relief in life without death. No peace, no power, no hope. The Elders are not angry because they've been put to sleep. They're apoplectic over being awaken. For the immortal, sleep is as close to freedom as they can get. Sleep is the great escape. The Warm Oblivion. Cthulhu doesn't emerge from R'lyeh triumphant. The immaculate chaos isn't by design or indicative of a cosmic consciousness. Cthulhu's rage is the reflexive response to being denied the illusion of death and a natural manifestation of his curse: His immortality. It's the pain of the Never Born."

My name is Sonny. I am an astronaut lost in space without hope of rescue, drifting in a fleshy protective coating–but I will never die. Driven insane by decades of isolation and back into sanity through thousands of tantric reactions, I've regressed into a zygote before re-expanding into an ancient monk. As wise as any human can be and yet still an infant in the Horse Eyes of the Mother. Portals to infinite dimensions are no cure for the crushing loneliness of immortality. Without the ultimate joy of sleep, every adventure is a struggle, every challenge is gargantuan, and every truth is a lie.

Humans fear death and dream of immortality. But for the immortal, fear of death is the ultimate eroticism. The idea of deep, endless sleep: Orgasmic.

God expanded and towered over me, red eyes blazing, huge toothy smile gleaming. His fingers elongated into tubes, and then further into needles. God punctured my skin with his needle fingers, pumping me full of intoxicating fluids both corrosive and soothing, elevating me to the highest heights of the Warm Oblivion. God filled my mind with images of lesser deities and monsters, dimensions both familiar and alien, a complete history of history.

There was a mighty earthquake followed by a hot rain and a sudden flood. Caught beneath the landslide, I was cast into the Underworld, immersed in a volcanic sludge that clung like tar. Black ooze filled my nostrils, throat, lungs... my every pore. The black ooze melted my cells, broke down my DNA, and left me a barely conscious puddle of putrescence. Like a seed struck by lightning, mitosis was initiated, then accelerated until chunks of substance emerged in the grotesque soup. Membranes burst forth with splendid tendrils, pulling coagulated clots into skin, teeth, and organs. There was pressure on all sides, pushing squishy bits into clumps that became limbs, eyes, and fingers. The pressure began to grow, as though my environment was dwindling, as though the gloomy wet universe was shrinking around me into a sphere the size of a grape.

A final, bloody explosion.

The Grim Finger Clanspeople pulled me from a steaming gash of earth. Two of the strongest held me upside down, each holding me up by an ankle. A third slapped my back with a fibrous plank as black tar gushed from my lungs and out my throat and nose. I screamed like I had never screamed before, like I was screaming for the first time. Another member of the tribe removed a fleshy vine running from my navel into the gash I'd just been pulled from. Then they tossed me onto a bed of moss and animal skins. The scales fell from my eyes. I was naked and fearless. The process had transformed me into an immortal. Unborn. I was blessed. And I was damned.

People are afraid of death. They fear the idea of an end to consciousness, an end to temporal reality, an unescapable blackness that offers neither comfort nor torment. They should be so lucky. Hell would be Nirvana by comparison to the reality of life never-ending, of joining forces with a single all-knowing consciousness.

My name is Sonny, and I am The Grim Finger Clanspeople. We exist underground at dizzying depths, surrounded by rocks both melted and crystalline, sustained by microscopic vegetation and mammoth beasts that roam the catacombs, servants of the one true God.

Our city is massive. Our city is alive. This Xanadu is also our Savior, an extension of the Ultimate. Our city is a beetle, the size of a planetoid, an ancient protector, an Adversary of light comprised of more colors than our spectrum can detect: An Immaculate Scarab. At intervals dictated by planetary alignments and the whims of God, our city travels, and all of us with it.

Before burrowing through tungsten tectonics, swimming vast oceans, and surfing active veins of molting lava, The Grim finger Clanspeople are packed like cargo. Beneath the glorious wings, within semi-porous craters, about the size and shape of coffins or futuristic hibernation pods. Each member of the tribe is encapsulated, encased in a milky, amber secretion that hardens before the city makes its maneuvers. Each member of the tribe enters a waking stasis, protected from the extremes of heat and cold, becoming one with the Great Insect's mighty armor, plugged into its vast and complex consciousness.

The city moves once a millennium or once a week, as cosmic forces and God's whims dictate. Before settling in the desert below Las Vegas the city lived miles beneath the streets of Budapest. Before that Siberia. Before that South Africa. There are times when the city settles so deep it's completely inaccessible—except by wormhole.

The population of the city grows and wanes, as dictated by the rotation of galaxies and the whims of God. Settlements have been scattered at every stop, and now number in the thousands. It's an entire world below the world, an atlas of counties and communities, each with their own unique cultural customs and mores. Yet each united by blood and consciousness. The individualities become part of the entirety until an individual only exists in concept, even as one draws in the mud and another explores virgin caverns. Every movement dictated by the gravitational influences of cosmic forces, tempered by the whims of God.

The city will be moving momentarily, in advance of the Greatest Conjunction Ever and confirmed by the will of God. I'll be led into a crevasse, entombed in the Scarab's nourishing lacquer. Like a pill in a blister-pack.

My surface self is a whisper, a subtle siren's song, one that beckoned me upwards with memories of the Sun. But even if it were possible to disconnect myself from the collective, to escape the rage of betrayal, the scores of predators, worms, and diseases, could I find my way back?

And what would await me? A decimated wasteland teaming with zombies and cannibals, maybe? Or a sky blackened by chemicals, patrolled by Overseers from Universe 25? Does the Moon still orbit above, or will shattered remnants be the only proof that it ever existed? The possibilities are infinite, and all of them, in their own unique way, are unacceptable.

Worst to contemplate: Would everything be exactly the same? The lights and bells of Vegas still creating hypnotic vibrations designed to separate lost souls from their worldly possessions? Would I still be a junkie, a criminal, a cast-off?

"Hey Sonny."

"Yeah Drew."

"Did I ever tell you about this lost tribe of Jews and the Cave of Letters?"

"Yeah, you did. Way back on that first night we met."

"Oh. Hey, did you know that Jews don't believe in Hell?"

"Actually, that's not true, Drew. Ancient Jews believed in a dark realm called Sheol. While modern interpretations describe it as a resting place for all the dead, the earliest Hebrew texts were very specific. Sheol is exclusively for the wicked dead, and when you live there, you become a wraith called a 'Rephaim,' an entity without any real personality or strength. The Bible mentions The Witch of Endor, a female magician who had tried, and failed, to talk to God by casting lots. Still, she found a way to contact Samuel for Saul when he was trapped in Sheol. Communing with the damned of Sheol was subsequently forbidden in Deuteronomy 18:10, effectively ending the common Jewish practice of communing with dead ancestors. Sheol became synonymous with Hades in ancient Greek texts, but you want to know something interesting, Drew? The thing that made Sheol 'Hell' wasn't flames or demons of torture. It was being separated from God, and from your friends. That's what Hell really is."

"Hey Sonny."

"Yeah Drew?"

"Did I ever tell you the story about when me and my best friend went on a pilgrimage to the center of the world?

"No, Drew. Tell me..."

Two junkies, sharing a dirty sleeping bag, grudgingly stoking a pathetic bonfire in the storm drains of Las Vegas.

"It was worth it."

EPILOGUE

[Recovered from the personal diary of Gina De-marco, Deceased]

I CAME TO LAS Vegas to find my brother, alive or dead.

If I can't find him, then I'm giving up. My psychiatrist says I've become obsessed. I'm destroying my life, pushing everyone away, and slowly killing myself. After all these years, it's time for me to find resolution. It's the first step towards dealing with my depression and guilt. It's something I need to do if I'm ever going to get healthy again. It's something I need to do in order to stop the nightmares.

My brother Sonny never came home from my husband's bachelor party. He didn't want to go in the first place. He said it wasn't his idea of a good time, and he had never really bonded with my then-fiancé. I told him it would mean the world to me if he could just try to be part of the family. I told him how important Jeremey was to me, and how I wanted them to feel like brothers. I also admitted that I was nervous about Jeremey going crazy for his last-bash, and I wanted Sonny on the ground as my eyes and ears. It was silly, I know. Petty and paranoid.

"I need you to make sure he doesn't fuck any strippers," I told him, coaxing a slight smile.

I'd do anything to take it back. I wish I'd never pressured him to go. Because he never came home.

Jeremey had no idea what had happened. He said that after an expensive dinner at the Bellagio, Sonny excused himself for a cigarette and never came back. They spent a couple of hours searching for him, but when they couldn't find him, they figured he'd just gone off to do his own thing. They were surprised when he missed the flight home the next afternoon.

I exploded at Jeremey when I heard. "Did you call the police? Did you call the hospitals? How could you abandon my brother?" Jeremey insisted he'd done what he thought was appropriate. It was no secret that Sonny had issues, that he was prone to debilitating bouts of melancholy. He'd disappeared before, only to resurface days later (usually filthy and dazed).

"Its just Sonny being Sonny," Jeremey responded. "He's probably doing it for attention because he doesn't want us to be happy."

Yeah, like Sonny would do anything to hurt me on purpose.

I spent the next two weeks frantically phoning authorities in Las Vegas, the staff at The Luxor, hospitals, homeless shelters... Nothing. I filled a missing person's report, sent out social media blasts, and even offered rewards for any information regarding Sonny's whereabouts. I was ready to call off the wedding, but Jeremey wouldn't hear of it.

"We can't let your brother's unacceptable behavior get in the way of our happiness," he insisted. "He's a grown-up and he's made his choice."

"And what choice was that?" I responded fiercely. "What aren't you telling me? What happened in Las Vegas?"

"Nothing!" he screamed. "I didn't even want him there. I only took him because you demanded it."

My wedding day was one of the saddest days of my life. I swallowed a fist-full of Xanax just so I'd be able to smile my way through it, pushing down my emotional agony. Instead of the beautiful dresses and tuxedos, the immaculate reception hall, the gathering of friends and loved ones, the gourmet dinner, all I saw was Sonny's absence. I hated the way everyone just pretended everything was normal—even my parents. "Wherever he is, I'm sure he's thinking about you," mom said with a vague shimmer of a tear in her eye. "Don't worry. He'll come home when he's ready. Just like he always does."

Except he didn't.

My honeymoon was a nightmare. Nine days in Maui and I couldn't leave my hotel room for more than an hour before losing my mind. I was a mess. Jeremey was beside himself. His frustration culminated on the fifth day when, after berating me for my failure to fuck him following our nuptials, he trashed the hotel room. We were evicted and had to spend the rest of our vacation in a cheap motel by the airport. Jeremey decided to spend the last few days in Maui by himself. We met at the airport and flew back without saying a word or even looking at each other.

Things only got worse. I just couldn't forgive myself for sending Sonny to Las Vegas, and I couldn't forgive Jeremey for losing him. I started to suspect Jeremey of something nefarious. I imagined him getting into an argument with Sonny and killing him. I had a nightmare about Sonny being set on fire and buried in the desert. I started thinking my husband was a sociopath, a Ted Bundy type with murderous designs. It wasn't long before I couldn't stand looking at him before his touch made me sick. I quit my job and fell into a deep, dark depression that felt utterly unescapable.

Jeremey had me committed!

But after a few days, I wasn't even mad at him anymore. Compared to dealing with him on a daily basis, the hospital was like a vacation. The drugs were amazing. All of my guilt and anxiety faded into a warm oblivion. I sat through hours of group therapy and intensive one-on-one sessions with Dr. Cunningham. Even though I was declared mentally stable after a month, I stayed for over a year.

The first thing I did upon my release was file for divorce. The second thing I did was hire a private investigator to find Sonny.

Darren Warwick was considered an expert in his field. He had established connections with official and underground sources in Las Vegas, enabling him to navigate the complex social hierarchies of the city. He spent two years on the case before I ran out of money.

He didn't find Sonny, obviously, but he was definitely on his trail. Warwick hit dead ends in the tunnels below the city. Sonny didn't have an arrest record, but Warwick found out my brother had connections with a local heroin dealer. He was a person of interest in a shooting police believed stemmed from a drug deal gone bad. There were rumors that Sonny had been involved in a swindle, running afoul of local cartel bosses. I didn't sound like the Sonny I knew, but Warwick insisted his intel was solid.

Sonny was born with his umbilical cord wrapped around his neck. His face was completely blue when he came out. They told my mom and his dad how lucky they were, that it didn't look like there would be any permanent damage. But you could tell that mom always suspected my brother was broken.

He was sickly, dyslexic, and hyperactive as a child. He had intense mood swings as an adolescent. He went from getting straight A's to nothing but D's and C's in High School. He was mildly agoraphobic. He was afraid of airplanes and believed in UFOs.

He only became more eccentric after going to Community College in Santa Cruz. He came home for Christmas with dreadlocks and covered in tattoos. When he wasn't around, his quirks were an endless source of prattle for mom, who regarded him with concern and consternation. She was embarrassed of him—she always had been.

I wasn't any better. I was a terrible big sis. It wasn't until after his first suicide attempt that I realized how sensitive and vulnerable he really was. And even though I grew fond of him, felt extremely protective of him, I was never his advocate. I never invited him out with me and my friends when we were kids, never spoke up for him when he was humiliated or abused. I hardly even kept in touch with him after I moved out.

Before he disappeared, I remember having a series of dreams about him, dreams where we were both weeping about an impending tragedy that couldn't be avoided. I thought, I don't know, that he was sending me vibrations—warning me that he was on the edge. This was my motivation for insisting that Jeremey take him along to Vegas for the bachelor party. I figured he'd be safest in a group, in a crowded environment. I had no idea he'd be cast out. I didn't realize how easily Vegas could swallow up someone like Sonny.

Every morning I'd make the rounds to all the jails, hospitals, and morgues. I looked at more John Does than anyone should have to.

I walked around the sleaziest areas of Old Las Vegas with a picture of Sonny, asking everyone and anyone if they'd seen him. At first, I was encouraged by the number of people who claimed to have seen him, until I realized those promising to have concrete info all wanted money for it. Those who were willing to talk for free told me outlandish and often conflicting stories.

I heard that Sonny was a major player in the heroin trade from some, and that he was an undercover cop who got what he had coming from others. I was told he won millions on a random spin of a roulette wheel, and that he was holed up in the Bellagio under an alias. One of the most common reports I got was that Sonny was living underground, in the sewers and storm drains that ran for miles beneath the city. I'd ask for specifics but was warned that the tunnels were no place for a pretty thing like myself.

People told me Sonny was under the protection and control of a well-known hustler named Andrew who, coincidentally, had also been missing for years.

And then I saw him.

Sonny was standing outside The Golden Nugget, smoking a cigarette and asking people for change. I almost fainted. He looked so ragged, with sunken eyes, a patchy beard, and long fingernails. I should have contained myself—I should have stayed back and watched him for a while. At the very least, I should have approached him slowly, cautiously.

Instead, I screamed "Sonny!" and ran straight towards him.

He didn't even seem to recognize me at first, but as I closed in on him, he got a look of abject terror on his face. Before I could grab his arm, he turned and bolted. I chased him for blocks, screaming and crying, telling him that I loved him.

Eventually, he turned down an alley and disappeared. By the time I caught up, he was gone. It was a dead end, so the only way he could have gotten away is if he had climbed up a fire escape or jumped down a solitary manhole.

I approached the cover-less hole and yelled into the hissing, humid darkness

"Sonny!"

Of course he didn't respond, but I heard voices down there. I ran to the closest convenience store and bought a flashlight, determined to follow those voices into the sewers and into Hell if that's what it took. But when I came back to the alley, the manhole was—gone. I know how ridiculous that sounds, but the manhole was gone. Not covered—gone, like it had never been there to begin with. And yes, I'm absolutely certain it was the same alley.

At least I was. Obviously, my conviction's faded. Maybe I just wanted to find Sonny so badly, I let myself believe things that weren't real.

That night, though, I had the most vivid, detailed dream of my life. I wasn't a participant in this dream, it was like I was watching a movie.

Sonny had transformed into some kind of comic book action hero. That's not really accurate, but I don't know how else to describe it. He looked healthy again, and he was on this adventure that was like a modern-day *Dungeons and Dragons* campaign.

He was smart and confident, not to mention strong and brave. The story didn't make sense. What I mean is, it wasn't linear and there was no context for anything. But Sonny was breaking out of dungeons and battling monsters. And then there were scenes that were like a sci-fi movie and scenes that were like a horror movie—and there were dream sequences. So, I was inside the dreams of someone who I was dreaming about. The entire story took place underground in a labyrinth beneath our feet that leads all the way to the center of the Earth, and each turn brings new wonders and terrors.

This dream seemed to last for hours.

Eventually, Sonny became the leader of an underground society, ruling over tens of thousands of subjects. As the world around them began to crumble, Sonny and his entire community took shelter inside this bio-mechanical machine. There's nothing I can compare it too, but it was like an arc of some sort, and it was designed to "sail" through solid ground and brimstone.

After a voyage that seemed to last months, the arc settled in a new location, thousands of miles away. They emerged into an immense, domed ceremonial coliseum where Sonny and his community were greeted by another King and his subjects. As the two Kings approached each other atop this huge alter, surrounded by thousands of combined subjects, a look of shock and then joy came over Sonny's face.

"Drew!" he exclaimed, "You're not dead!" And the two of them hugged and wept and their citizens erupted into cheers of joy and unity. An orchestra swelled as a portal opened in the center of the immense dome and a brilliant shaft of light illuminated the arena. I was flooded with emotions and woke up sobbing. I know how silly this sounds, but I felt so happy of Sonny—so proud of him. He'd endured so much in his life and now, he would be celebrated and exalted. There was no more pain for Sonny—ever.

It was just a dream. I know this. I'm not saying I have ESP or that this is what I believe happened to my brother. Still, I'd been transformed by the experience, because it was more than a dream, it was a vision. I had found my peace—my center.

My guilt and fears all melted away. I accept that I will probably never know what happened to Sonny. And I'm okay with that. I jumped out of bed, threw opened the curtains and looked up at the orange sky. I just couldn't stop smiling.

And this intense, intoxicating feeling of contentment didn't just put my heart at ease in regard to Sonny, but in regard to everything.

I'm still riding that high, and now, even the realities of civil unrest, crumbling infrastructures, and impending doom seem like minor annoyances. And as for the choice I've been struggling with since the Fall, it all seems crystal clear now.

Jeremey sent me a coded message yesterday: He is pledging his support to The Basilisk on the eve of the Great Tuning—but I won't be.

I'll be hopping a shuttle to the outer colonies to join the resistance.

ABOUT THE
AUTHOR

Over the past decade-plus, Joshua Millican has proven himself to be a horror expert of the highest caliber. After establishing a personal blog in 2011, Millican quickly became one of the genre's premiere journalists, contributing to many websites before ultimately landing at Dread Central in 2016. One of the top horror outlets on the planet, Millican served as Editor-in-Chief from 2019 through 2021. In addition to writing, Millican has been a member of numerous festival juries, a popular podcast guest, and has even scored a handful of acting gigs. His talk show *Chronic Horror* (sidelined by the Pandemic) explored the intersection of horror movie fandom and cannabis culture. Now married and a father for the first time, Millican is excited to pen more hardcore horror/ sci-fi/fantasy fiction for Encyclopocalypse Publications.

Follow Joshua Millican on Twitter at @josh_millican.